MONSTERS

BLACK

MONSTERS

BLACK

D.R. Mills

SEA OF INK PRESS

MONSTERS
BLACK

Cover: MiblArt
Interior book design: Enchanted Ink Publishing
Editing: A. P. Mobley at Sea of Ink Press

The text type was set in Minion Pro.

ISBN: 979-8-9874347-2-7 (Paperback)

For Bandit

You were this man's first best friend.

D.R. MILLS
PRESENTS . . .

MONSTERS

PROLOGUE

SHAWNTELL BLAKE MOMENTARILY LOWERED her paintbrush from the canvas to reach over and scratch her right arm. She'd had a strange rash on it for the past two days–ever since they'd gotten rid of that damn *dog*.

She sighed as she sat on a stool in her art studio, rain pelting the window beside her. That was life this time of year in Twilight Peak. Sometimes the spring brought sunny weather, and other times it brought rain showers that lasted for days.

She moved her bright-red bangs away from her glasses with her paintbrush handle and peered outside. Her husband and their daughter stood in the downpour next to an empty doghouse. Shawntell huffed at the sight. *Those morons are going to catch their deaths out there.*

Using her brush handle again, she readjusted her glasses and turned back to her canvas.

She was working on a self-portrait this time, and she'd been doing a perfect job–as always. She glanced in the mirror next to the easel before dipping her brush in white and applying a touch of the color to the picture.

Her studio was in full view behind her, but she hadn't planned on adding a detailed background to her self-portrait. Various pieces painted by her own magnificent hand were framed all over the scarlet walls. Old easels, spare utensils, and a small sink had been set against the wall to her right, while more equipment and tools lay on the desk to her left.

The sound of rain hitting glass was hypnotizing, and soon Shawntell slipped back into her element. A gorgeous image resided somewhere inside of her, and she intended to bring it to the surface. To bring it to life.

She mixed white with orange so she could add the lighter parts of her hair. As she touched up the finer details, the rash on her arm began to furiously itch. Again.

She sighed in frustration, set her utensil down, and raked her nails up and down her skin. *What is with this thing? Itching cream doesn't help it. Scratching doesn't help it. At this rate, I could lop off my arm and it still wouldn't go away.*

For the eighth time in the past hour, she raised her limb to the light to inspect it. The rash presented itself in several red dots that formed a zigzag shape, almost like a bite mark, and it was surrounded by pink skin. It had started burning, too. Probably because she was constantly scratching it. *That mangy beast is lucky it didn't bite me. I must have developed an allergy to it– that's probably why my skin is so irritated. Thank God it's finally dead.*

Shrugging off her thoughts, Shawntell fixed her posture and resumed her work. For now she would just have to deal with the discomfort.

She got in a few more brush strokes before the door behind her opened. "Linda and I are going to the hospital to see AJ," her husband, Aaron, said quietly.

She glanced at him through the mirror. He was soaked from head to toe, his jet-black hair matted to his forehead in sopping strands, his short beard dripping with little beads of water. He wore jeans, a tank top, and a zip-up hoodie–definitely not an outfit built for this weather.

Shawntell turned back to her work. "You sure you don't want to go stand in the rain for another fifteen minutes?"

Aaron paused before replying. "You know what we were doing out there."

"Did you bury the mutt near my rose garden at least? He'd finally be useful for something."

"Are you coming with us or not?" The question was laced with irritation.

Shawntell dabbed her brush with more paint and continued stroking. "Go ahead without me."

Aaron shoved the door all the way open and stomped inside. "Your *son* is in the hospital and you'd rather sit here and paint?"

Shawntell whirled around to face him. "It's not *my fault* he's in the hospital. It's *yours*. Don't you dare try to guilt-trip me. I've already been up there a few times these past two days. He's going to be all right. So instead of moping around and acting like he's not, I'm going to do what I do best." She set her brush down and scratched her arm again.

Aaron remained silent, staring at her intently. It was as if he'd only just realized whom he'd married. *Hopefully I've refreshed his memory.*

She grabbed the brush again and waved Aaron away. "You can go now."

He hung his head, stepped out of the room, and closed the door.

With peace restored, Shawntell spun around to face her art and resumed painting. The absolute *nerve* of that man to suggest she should feel bad for what had occurred–well, it was ridiculous. She loved her son, but the responsibility rested squarely on Aaron's shoulders. She had been inside sketching when it happened.

After a few moments, she heard a car door slam shut, and an engine roared to life. Headlights glared through her window as Aaron and Linda pulled out of the driveway.

Finally, they drove off. *Good riddance. Now there are no distractions. Just me, and me.* She topped off the left side of her cheek with another layer of paint before cleaning and drying her brush, then scooted back a bit to scan her work. Something about the hair was still off...

It needs more red, she realized, snapping her fingers. Leaning in, she mixed the color and applied it to the ends of the painting's ginger curls. The more she worked, the better it looked.

Her rash burned still. In fact, it seemed to be getting worse somehow. As she prepared to scratch herself in vain, a foul odor overcame the familiar scent of paint. She stifled a gag, covering her nose. *What the hell is that?* Whatever it was, it reminded her of dogs, and she *hated* dogs. Their smells, their drool, their dopey, lost little faces.

Shrill barking came from outside, and she peered out her window. A puppy with all black fur stood in her backyard. She recognized the little pest right away. It had been hanging around her house for the past two days–ever since the mutt died.

"Get lost, you rodent!" She slapped the glass, and the puppy scampered into the doghouse. *I can smell that stupid stray all the way in here. Either that, or the mutt is stinking up his own grave.* She turned on her fan, then picked up her brush and looked in the mirror.

What she saw in the reflection made her blood run cold.

A large dark figure with glowing maroon eyes loomed over her from behind. It was dog-shaped, but other than that, it didn't possess many discernible features. Smoke swirled out from beneath its "paws," a vicious growl escaping its throat.

Pulse quickening, she spun around to face the beast. A black shadow obscured her vision.

Shawntell screamed as something sharp sank deep into her neck. White-hot pain seared through her body, and she glanced down to see claws as they ripped through her flesh. The dog-like creature tore her from the stool onto the floor.

She tried to shove the monster away. It was too powerful. Soon the strength in her arms faded, and waves of terror and agony swept her into darkness.

BLACK

CHAPTER 1

WILLY SPRINTED THROUGH THE RAIN. The downpour had eased in the night, but it was coming down hard again this afternoon.

He ran past Ryan's house, then up the hill toward Chyann's place, his shoes splashing through puddle after puddle. Finally, he made it to the driveway and hastened to the front door. But when he turned the knob and pushed in, the door wouldn't budge. *Oh, come on*, he thought, and knocked furiously.

A moment later, the handle *click*ed. The door opened, and Chyann peered out from behind it. Willy hurried inside. "Jeez, Chy," he said, trembling from the cold. "I could'a caught my death out there."

She shut the door behind them. "I should be so lucky. Maybe then I'd get my homework done."

Willy narrowed his eyes at her. "Who does homework on the weekend?"

Chyann walked past him and headed up the stairs. "Trust me, I'd rather be doing anything else right now." Willy kicked off his wet sneakers and followed her. "Besides," she continued as she reached the top of the staircase, "right now is the only time I have to do it."

She rounded the corner and made it into her room, then grabbed a towel from her bathroom and handed it to Willy once he reached her side. He took it and started drying off. "You're a smarty-pants, anyway. You don't need to do homework to keep up in class."

"No." She crossed her arms. "But I *do* need to do it to keep up my GPA."

Willy plopped down onto a beanbag chair and shook his head. "Nerd." Chyann rolled her eyes and sat down at her desk. As she resumed her work, Willy wrapped the towel around his shoulders and asked, "You heard from Ry yet?"

"Not since yesterday after school," she replied, scribbling something onto her paper. "Why?"

"You think he's been a little off lately?"

"He went through a lot last week, so yeah. He doesn't exactly have a 'normal' anymore."

Willy clenched a fist, recalling the severe beating Steve Helsing had given his friend. "You think we're ever gonna see Helsing again?"

Chyann paused for a long time before answering. "I hope not."

Another few minutes passed. Footsteps sounded outside of Chyann's room. Ryan wandered inside, pulling his hood over his head.

Willy's stomach twisted as he took in the bruises and cuts riddling Ryan's face. The boy was well on his way to healing up, as his injuries looked much better than the last time Willy had seen him, but they were still noticeable. He had a butterfly bandage on the bridge of his nose, his bottom lip and his left brow split open.

Ryan stopped near Chyann's desk. "Good, you're both here."

Chyann lowered her pencil. "What's up?"

"You seen the news yet?"

Willy perked up in his seat. "We got somethin'?"

Ryan nodded. "I think so."

Chyann started typing away at her laptop. She pulled up an article online, then leaned in and read it out loud. "Local woman brutally mauled to death inside locked home."

"Fun stuff," Willy said, twisting the ends of his towel.

Chyann continued. "Last night, local artist Shawn-tell Blake was home alone when she was attacked in her studio by an unknown animal. By the time she was found, it was too late. Authorities aren't sure what type of animal it was, or how it entered the premises."

Willy craned his head to examine the news article. *Did I hear that right?* Chyann kept scrolling, and Willy caught an image of a redheaded woman with thick-rimmed glasses. His heart fell at the sight, and he leaned back, sinking into the beanbag. *Shit.*

"This sucks to hear," Chyann said sadly.

Ryan furrowed his brow. "Have you met her?"

"No, I haven't," Chyann admitted. "But I've seen her work, and I'm pretty sure I've got a class with her daughter." Willy tried to relax. *Could be worse, I guess.*

"I think it's worth checking out," Ryan said. "It sounds like our brand of weird."

Chyann turned to Ryan. "For Will and I, maybe. You're still recovering."

Ryan shrugged. "I'm fine."

Chyann raised a brow. "Are you?"

"Yeah, I am. And I'm bored. I've been sitting around doing nothing for the past week since my mom took me out of school." He gestured at her computer. "How do you think I found out about this? I was watching the *news*."

Chyann tilted her head and glanced at Willy, and Willy pointed at Ryan. "He's got a point."

Her stare trailed back to the screen. After a while of silence, she looked at Ryan again. "Fine. You can come."

Ryan stuffed his hands into his jacket pockets. "Okay then. Let's go." He left the room. Chyann sighed, powered off her computer, and slid her papers to the side.

Willy climbed to his feet. "Don't worry, Chy. Homework is overrated anyway." He dropped the towel on her chair and followed after Ryan.

Chyann said something to Willy, but he didn't hear what. He was thinking about the Blake family. *Figures. Out of all the people in Twilight Peak that evil could pick on, it had to be* her *family.*

This was going to suck.

*C*HYANN PUT THE CAR IN PARK, RAIN STEADILY beating against the top of the vehicle. Her mom had bought the used car for her a few days before the rain had started, which was a saving grace for Willy, considering he'd already been in the rain today.

He sat in the back seat, leaning forward to better see the street of homes ahead of them. The Blake house was three buildings up on the left.

"Is that it?" Chyann asked, gesturing at the building.

Ryan double-checked his phone. "Yeah, that's our house."

Chyann tilted her head as she peered through the window. "Is anybody home?"

"Nah," Willy answered. "We should be good." There was a pause, and his friends turned around to give him confused stares. *Crap!* he thought. *Did I sound too sure?* He pointed at the driveway. "Two-car driveway, guys. One car is gone, and the other probably belongs to the victim, right?"

There was another pause as they considered his words. Finally, Chyann spoke. "I guess that's a good point." She turned and shared one more look with Ryan. The two of them shrugged.

Willy sighed, relaxing. *Close one.*

"The front door is pretty exposed," Ryan said. "Maybe there's a back one we can try? One that's hidden from the neighbors?"

Chyann opened the door and climbed out of the car. "If we're lucky, yeah." Ryan and Willy followed her lead. Together, they hurried down the street.

They crept through the yard of the closest house, then into the alleyway connecting all the buildings on one side. Walking down the paved path dug up some old memories for Willy, but he attempted to drive them from his mind as he and his friends stopped at the Blake house. A short white fence stood between them and the place's small backyard, and when Willy laid his eyes on the area, it was hard for him to ignore the feelings rising in his chest. *It looks exactly the same.* There had been many times he'd hopped this fence, just as Ryan and Chyann were doing now, and each time his heart had raced at the thought of seeing *her*.

A little over a year had passed since he'd last been here.

"Will, hurry up." Chyann's voice snapped him out of his trance. He looked up to see her and Ryan waving him over to the back door.

Willy trudged past a dumpster, gripped the gate-post, and swung himself over the fence. As he jogged over to his friends, he noticed the empty doghouse to his right, then a fresh mound of dirt under the tree to his left. A wooden cross had been erected atop the mound. A worn dog collar hung from the cross, and its tag read *Buddy*.

Willy's heart fell to his feet. He slowed to a stop. *Buddy died? What happened?*

Ryan waved at Willy. "Dude, hurry up before somebody sees us."

Willy shook his head and hurried to the back porch. "Sorry, I'm on it." He retrieved his lockpicks from his sweatshirt and went to work.

"What's with you today?" Ryan asked. "You've been acting weird ever since we left Chy's place."

"I'm hungry, man," Willy lied. "You know I can't think clearly when my stomach's growlin.'"

15

"Then we're gonna have to start packing you snacks when we break into places."

Willy smirked. "Why do that when I can just eat something inside?"

"No," Chyann cut in sternly.

Several seconds ticked by, and the lock *click*ed. Willy opened the door and motioned for his friends to head inside. Before he followed them in, a dark shadow flashed across the edges of his vision.

He spun around and scanned his surroundings. Nothing seemed out of place.

After taking a final glance at Buddy's grave, Willy entered the house and closed the door.

The inside of the Blake home was as painfully familiar as the outside, but some things looked different from the last time Willy had visited. For instance, it appeared the kitchen had been rearranged.

Chyann and Ryan wandered through the room, searching for clues. "We're looking for her art studio, right?" Chyann asked.

Ryan nodded, rubbing the side of his head with a slight wince. "The article said she was found there."

"Got it." Chyann walked down the hallway to the right. "Basement, maybe?" Willy knew that hall would lead her into the living room. He inched over to the short hall on the left and peered down it. Between him and the front door up ahead was another door. Yellow caution tape had been plastered across it. *Maybe they won't think it's weird that I found it so quick?*

Willy looked back at them. "Over here, amigos." He stepped into the hall and stopped next to the door, glancing over the family portraits on the walls. Some had been painted, while others had been profession-ally taken, and Shawntell was prominent in each and every one. Her smile made her seem gentle and kind, but Willy knew better.

The knowledge that Shawntell had been killed was conflicting for him. She was a huge bitch, sure, but she probably didn't deserve whatever had happened to her. *Probably.*

Next, he gazed at her husband, Aaron, in the pic-tures. Willy didn't know him very well, but he seemed like a stand-up guy. In Willy's time around the Blakes, he'd spoken to Aaron the least, but their conversations hadn't been bad.

Willy's eyes fell from the parents to the children. Linda and her little brother, AJ, were either sitting or standing next to their parents in every photo. Both had Aaron's jet-black hair. Linda was the same age as Willy and his friends, but AJ was three years younger than them.

Poor AJ…

Willy knew how close the boy had been to the fam-ily dog, Buddy. Between Shawntell's death and whatever happened to the dog, Willy suspected AJ wasn't doing very well.

Willy turned to see Ryan and Chyann as they rounded the corner and approached the studio door.

"Should we be worried about fingerprints?" Chyann asked.

Ryan shook his head. "Nah, they've been over the scene already. Unless they comb through everything a second time, I think we're okay." Ryan reached for the knob. "Let's see what we've got." He opened the door.

Nothing could have prepared Willy to see the state the room was in.

Paint of all shades and rust-colored pools of dried blood coated the floor. Shelves had been knocked loose from the walls, lying broken and useless. Unfinished and ruined canvases were torn apart, splattered with paint and bodily fluids. Based on the roughly human-shaped hole in the mess of paint and blood, Willy had an idea of where Shawntell had been found.

For what felt like forever, he and his friends stared at the room. Chyann kept a hand over her mouth, but no one made a sound.

"So," Willy began, breaking the tense silence, "this must be the opposite of a 'happy accident.'"

Ryan tentatively stepped inside, avoiding the mess on the floor. "This place is a bloodbath..."

Willy followed Ryan inside, trying to be mindful of

where he placed his feet. "Yeah, and a blue, yellow, and green bath too."

"We get it," Chyann said quietly.

Willy found a corner mostly untouched by the chaos and stayed there, examining his surroundings. A fallen self-portrait of Shawntell stared at him from across the room, still attached to the easel. Blood had been flecked and smeared across the front, while the side touching the floor was stained by the now-dry puddle of gore it sat in.

"Do you guys smell that?" Chyann asked, scrunching her nose as she stood in the doorway.

Willy took a deep breath, trying to detect whatever Chyann had caught a whiff of. He hadn't noticed it before, but there was a faint scent he couldn't identify.

Ryan sniffed. "Smells like something's burning."

Willy inhaled again. "You're right. It's like, uhh… burnt wood?"

"I'm not sure," Chyann remarked.

As they began their search for the scent's source, Willy moved closer to where Shawntell had been found. Once he was as close as he could get without stepping in the muck, he knelt down.

Based on where her unfinished self-portrait lay, and the stool next to her body print, Willy guessed she'd been working before the attack. *What the hell happened here?*

"Guys," Chyann called from behind him. Willy looked back to see she'd finally entered the room. She was kneeling the same way he was, in the same place he'd been a few moments before.

Willy stood and carefully walked to her side. Ryan did the same. Soon they all stood together, staring down at what Chyann found.

Black scorch marks peeked out from underneath the dried paint and blood before their feet.

Chyann grabbed a craft knife from the floor and stuck the blade into the paint. She scraped away until they could see what was hidden.

A large paw print with long claws stained the wood of the floor.

Chyann set the knife aside, and Boss appeared in a flash over the left half of Ryan's face.

Willy could hardly believe what he was seeing. "Is that *burned* into the floor?"

Chyann crossed her arms. "Looks like it."

"What kind of creature does something like this?" Ryan asked.

Boss shook his half-head. "I have no idea…"

A pit formed in Willy's stomach. For once he had nothing witty to say. *Whatever this thing is, it's definitely our problem now.*

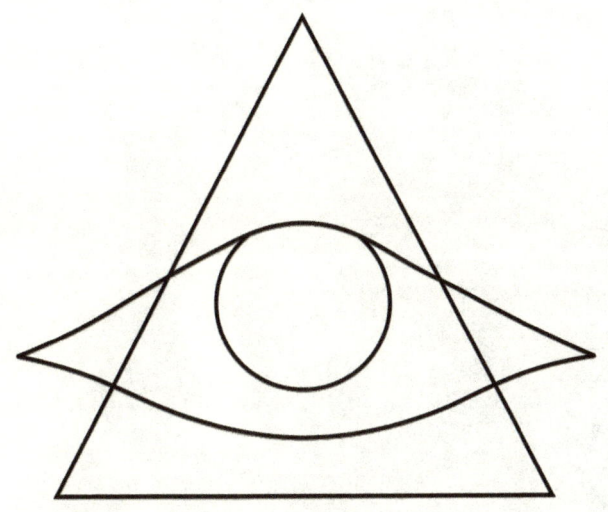

CHAPTER 2

THE HOSPITAL SMELLED OF ALCOHOL and sanitizer, and Linda hated it. In fact, she hated everything here, period.

She cradled her head in her hands and tried to hold back her sobs, tears soaking her palms. *This is too much...*

She heard a door open and lifted her head. Her father exited AJ's room and turned to her, looking down at her with puffy red eyes. He rubbed his cheeks and trudged toward her.

Linda opened her mouth, wanting to speak with her father, but no sound came out.

He took a seat in the chair next to her and released a long breath. "AJ's awake. I told him about your mother... and about Buddy."

Linda lowered her gaze to the floor. *So that's it, then. And if it weren't for me, we wouldn't be here in the first place.*

"He doesn't remember much," her dad continued. "If you want to talk to him before we leave, you can."

Although Linda wasn't sure whether she could handle talking to AJ right now, she rose from her seat, her knees weak and wobbly, and shambled across the hall to his room.

She stepped into the room. The lights were turned down low, the curtains drawn to keep the sun's bright rays at bay.

AJ lay still in bed, turned away from the door and facing the window. His shaggy black hair peeked out from the bandages that covered his head, his right leg elevated and wrapped in a cast. Even in the dim light, Linda could see the tears slipping down his cheeks.

She hugged her arms to her chest. "Hey."

AJ sniffed. "Dad said I got hit by a car."

Linda nodded. It was suddenly hard to breathe. "Yeah, you and Buddy both."

A long time passed before AJ spoke again. Finally, he faced Linda. "Did he suffer?"

She hung her head. *What am I supposed to say to that?* "No, he… he went pretty soon after it happened."

AJ closed his eyes and turned back to the window. "I didn't even get to say goodbye… to him, or to Mom."

Linda sat at his bedside. "He's buried under the tree in the backyard. When you get out of here, you can go and see him whenever you want."

AJ laughed once. "I guess." He wiped his tears away with the back of his hand.

Linda wanted to comfort him, but she hesitated. *If he knew the whole story, he wouldn't be talking to me right now.* She rested a palm on his arm and gave him a gentle squeeze. *I should tell him. I should...*

She licked her lips and cleared her throat. "Dad and I are going home to grab food and some other things for you. Gimme a list and I promise I'll bring you whatever you need."

AJ sucked down a few breaths and glanced over at her. "Can you bring me something of Buddy's? Something that'll just... make me feel like he's here with me?"

Immediately, Linda knew what she'd bring back for AJ. She smiled. "I think I have an idea for that, yeah."

Fresh tears streamed down AJ's cheeks. "Thanks, sis."

Linda gave him another squeeze. "Don't mention it." She got up and hurried to the door. "We'll be back soon." Glancing over her shoulder, she saw him offer her a sad smile.

The sight made her feel as though her heart were in a vice.

She slipped out into the hall.

Dad gave her a curious look. "Done already?"

"For now," Linda responded. "I need to get some things for him."

Her father sighed, and for the first time today, Linda noticed just how tired he appeared, his shoulders slumped, dark circles forming under his eyes. *Honestly*, she thought, *I doubt I look much better.*

He stood up from his seat and said, "I'll let the doctor know we'll be gone for a bit."

"Okay. I'll wait here."

As he headed down the hall, Linda leaned against the wall behind her and gazed through the window that led into AJ's room. Even though the blinds had been drawn, she could see her little brother through a small crack in them. He had his back to her, and he twitched every few seconds. Linda's eyes grew watery as she realized he must be weeping. *This is all my fault...*

Suddenly her arm started to itch. The sensation came on so strongly and abruptly that the limb jerked.

Trying to ease the irritation, she scratched her arm. However, her sweater was in the way, so she pulled the sleeve up to her elbow and scratched some more.

After raking her nails up and down her skin several times, the itch finally went away. *What the hell was that about?*

She lifted her arm to the light to look closer. A rash was forming on her forearm, turning her otherwise pinkish skin red. Raised dots had formed atop the irritated flesh in a zigzag pattern.

Linda's breath caught in her throat. *Isn't this the same rash Mom had before…*

She yanked her sleeve back down over her arm and shook her head. She'd surely caught the rash from her mother, but it was probably nothing, right? Nothing to freak out over, at least.

It's just a rash. Quit working yourself up over nothing. But no matter how many times she told herself that, she couldn't stop the dread from welling up in her stomach.

She couldn't help but feel afraid.

WILLY OPENED HIS MOUTH WIDE AND TOOK A huge bite of his burger. Ketchup and a few pickles fell out from the bottom. They plopped down onto his plate as he pulled his bite free and began chewing.

It was official. Larry made the best burgers in town.

After a long Saturday morning of running around town in the rain, Willy, Ryan, and Chyann stopped at their favorite diner, Larry's, for some lunch. Twilight Peak was old-fashioned, and Larry's was no different.

It looked like a diner straight out of the fifties, complete with checkered tile floors, red leather booths, and an old jukebox set into the far wall. The owner and head cook, Larry, specialized in burgers, milkshakes, and other stereotypical foods you'd expect a restaurant like his to serve.

Willy's favorite part about this place, though? Larry liked Willy and his friends. So much so that they often received meals on the house just for stopping in often and never causing trouble. *There ain't a place in town that's got Larry's beat*, Willy thought.

As he took another sloppy bite of his burger, he glanced over at Chyann. She sat next to him, picking fries off Ryan's plate while she read through more news articles on her phone. Ryan was halfway done with a burger of his own in the seat across from them.

Chyann finished chewing a fry and took another one. "So, what burns a paw print into the floor like that?"

Ryan shook his head and swallowed his bite. "No idea. I don't remember seeing anything in my grandpa's old books about something that can."

Willy wiped his face with the back of his hand, then snatched one of the pickles from his plate and popped it into his mouth. "Gotta be one hot dog to do it, right? Maybe our monster's a hellhound."

Chyann lowered her phone and looked at Ryan. He tilted his head, mulling over the idea. "Hellhounds are usually more like guard dogs, I think. They go after people who make deals with demons. You know, to collect souls and stuff."

Chyann grabbed a few more fries. "So maybe Shawntell made a deal with a demon?"

Willy scoffed. "Yeah, sure. What did she want? To be a good artist?"

"Maybe, yeah." Chyann shrugged.

Willy shook his head and went in for another bite of his burger. "She got ripped off then." He'd never been a fan of Shawntell, and the feeling had been mutual. She'd turned up her nose at him every time they'd been in a room together, and insulting her art was Willy's way of getting under her skin. It wasn't hard to make digs at her, either, considering he didn't understand why everyone liked her work so much. Mouth half full, he added, "I could'a drawn better with a couple'a crayons than she did with her whole art studio."

"If it *is* hellhounds," Ryan started, "there should be signs of some kind. Demonic omens."

Chyann furrowed her brow. "Demonic omens?"

"Dead flowers, swarms of flies, sulfur–things like that. Weird stuff that means something big and bad is hanging around."

"I don't remember anything like that in the house earlier," Chyann remarked.

Willy finished his burger and leaned back in the booth. "Me neither."

"Okay," Ryan said. "Then maybe we need to go back and have another look around."

Chyann crossed her arms. "Will and I can go."

Ryan paused, confused. "I said I was fine."

"And I believe you," she replied. "I just don't want you overdoing it."

Ryan wiped his face with a napkin and tossed it onto the plate. "I'm not overdoing anything. I haven't even *done* anything."

Chyann offered him a sunny smile. "Great. Let's keep things easy for you, then. Why don't you head home and go through those books for more info? Will and I can check out the house again and meet up with you later."

"Really?" Ryan said, chuckling. "You're sticking me on research duty?"

Chyann stole one last fry from his plate before scooting out of the booth. "Consider it payback for always sticking *me* with your guys' homework." She turned to Willy and gestured for him to follow her. "Let's go."

Willy winked at Ryan. "See ya when we get back, book-boy." He scrambled out of the booth and followed Chyann toward the diner's exit.

"You guys are jerks!" Ryan called after them.

Sorry buddy, Willy thought as he stepped outside. *Between a stack of books and the Blake house, I'll take my chances with the Blakes.*

*T*HE RAIN HADN'T EASED UP AT ALL SINCE THEIR trip to the Blake house earlier that day. In fact, it seemed to Willy that it was pouring even harder now. *It's been, like, three days. Is this stupid rain ever gonna stop?*

He and Chyann walked down the same alleyway as before, but this time they used the opposite end of the path so they wouldn't risk being spotted across neighboring lawns. Thankfully, they didn't have much farther to go until they reached their destination.

Willy ran a hand through his wet mohawk. "You sure it's best to ditch Ry with the books?"

Chyann shrugged. "I don't think he's ready for any action yet."

"Suddenly *you're* in charge of the monster-hunting association?"

"Hey," Chyann said, stopping. "Do you want him to get better or do you want him to get hurt again?"

"I want him to do a backflip while juggling a couple flaming chainsaws." After a pause he grinned. "C'mon, of course I want him to get better."

Chyann started toward the house again. "He won't get better if he doesn't take it easy."

Willy stuffed his hands into his sweater pocket and

scurried to her side. "Yeah, like Ry's gonna take it easy whenever there's a monster on the loose."

As they neared the Blakes' backyard, the gate opened. A young woman with jet-black hair that fell to her shoulders stepped out to drop a bag of trash into the dumpster. Willy's stomach dropped. *Oh, great.*

Linda Blake turned. When she saw Willy, she halted, her expression morphing into that of surprise. She stared at him with wide eyes, her deep-green irises almost hidden beneath her bangs.

"Willy?" Linda said as he slowed to a stop. She looked at Chyann momentarily before focusing on him.

Willy sighed. "Linda." Chyann glanced between the two of them several times. *The jig is up*, he thought. *Great.*

Linda hovered outside the open gate, and Willy noticed she was holding something in her free hand: Buddy's collar. "What are you doing here?" she asked, crossing her arms.

"We're, uhh…" He trailed off. *Need an excuse, need an excuse, need an excuse! Think Wylee, think!* He remembered Buddy's collar. "We're lookin' for my, um, dog."

Linda raised a brow. "Your dog?"

"Yeah." Willy laughed, shaking his head. He glanced over at Chyann, then turned back to Linda. "Little scamp is a damn escape artist. Loves to run."

Linda was quiet for several moments. "Is it a black puppy?" she asked.

Willy paused. *I guess I'll roll with it.* "Uhh, yeah, yeah. How'd you know?"

"'Cause it's been hanging around my yard for the past few days."

"Oh, really?" Willy leaned over to gaze into the yard. "I bet Buddy isn't too fond of that, huh?"

Linda didn't respond, and when Willy looked at her again, she gave him a suspicious stare. Her bottom lip quivered, and she said, "Buddy is… no longer with us."

Willy furrowed his brow, feigning confusion. "What?" He pretended to only now notice the collar. "*Oh.*" He rubbed the back of his head. "What happened?"

Linda lowered her left arm and scratched her wrist. "There was a car accident. He and AJ were…" She didn't finish her sentence, her voice cracking. Eventually, she continued. "AJ is in the hospital."

Willy stuffed his hands back into his sweater pocket. "Rough."

She kept scratching. "It's been a lot. Between that and my mom."

"I saw that, yeah. Sorry. You guys are really goin' through it right now."

"We'll survive. Somehow."

Willy smiled. "Somehow."

Chyann elbowed Willy in the side. "I didn't know you two knew each other."

"We've met once or twice," Willy replied. Chyann gave him a look that meant she expected an explanation later, then turned to Linda. "I'm so sorry about your mom. I saw some articles about it today. Sounds like it was really bad."

Linda crossed her arms again. "Thanks, Chy. It's been awful."

"Did the cops say anything about what they think it could have been?" Chyann asked.

Linda shook her head sadly. "They don't have a clue. Their best guess is some kind of wolf. But they don't even know how it got in the house yet."

Willy took a tentative step forward. "What about you? Did ya notice anything off the night it happened?"

Linda started scratching her arm some more. "Off how?"

"Smells, sounds, anything like that. Maybe it was already in the house or somethin.'"

Linda seemed to think about this for a bit. "Not that I can remember, no. My mom kept complaining about some bad smells the day before, though, and about that puppy hanging around the yard. But I never smelled or heard anything."

Willy and Chyann shared a knowing look. *Good enough for me*, he thought.

"I gotta get back to my dad," Linda said. She smiled at Chyann, then gave Willy the side-eye and headed back into her yard. "It was nice talking to you guys."

"Yeah," Willy replied. "You, too."

Linda furiously scratched her arm and disappeared from sight, and Willy spun on his heel and started back down the alley.

Chyann jogged up next to him and hit him on the arm. "Dude, what the hell was that?"

"Dunno what you're talkin' about."

"I'm talking about you and *Linda Blake* having this awkward tension. She's an honor roll student, and she's in my English class. How do you even know her?"

"We've talked," Willy admitted. "Little bit in the halls and stuff."

Chyann glanced over her shoulder at Linda's house. "Yeah, like *you* just casually talk to girls in the halls." She faced forward again, wearing a puzzled expression, before finally her jaw dropped. "Wait, were you two a *thing*?"

Willy avoided her gaze. "Oh, shut up."

Before Chyann could grill him, a yipe sounded from behind them. Willy stopped and turned around to see a black puppy in the center of the paved alley. It appeared to be a German Shepherd-Great Dane mix. It yiped at them a few more times before spinning around and running away. Then it leapt through a gap in the fence, vanishing into the Blakes' backyard.

Willy pointed. "That must be the puppy that's been hangin' around their place."

"Maybe it's got something to do with Shawntell?" Chyann suggested.

"Yeah," Willy said. "Maybe."

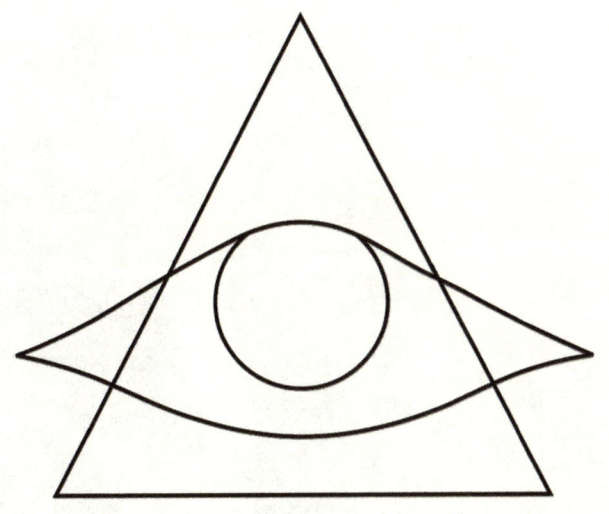

CHAPTER 3

CHYANN TEASED WILLY ALL THE WAY BACK to her house, and once they met up with Ryan, she got him in on it, too. Now they were trying to pry more information about Linda out of Willy as they hung out in Chyann's room.

"I told you guys," Willy began sternly, "she used to buy the snacks I was selling outta my locker. Remember how much bank I made off all those sodas and sweet cakes?"

Chyann laughed. "Yeah, right. Like that's all it is."

"C'mon," Willy whined. "You really think that if her and I got together, I'd be hidin' it like this?"

Ryan shook his head. "We know you wouldn't. That's why we're so curious."

Willy finished dabbing his neck with a towel before he tossed it aside and leaned back against the beanbag chair he sat in. "You guys are relentless, you know that?" Ryan and Chyann just kept staring at him, grins on their lips. It was becoming painfully apparent to him that if he didn't give them the truth about Linda, they were never going to stop asking about it. He sighed in frustration. "All right, fine. Yeah, we dated for a few weeks last year. Happy?"

"A few *weeks*?" Chyann shouted. "So you guys weren't just talking? You actually *dated*? Are you serious?"

Willy shrugged. "She's into bad boys."

"How come you never told us?" Ryan asked.

Willy scratched his cheek. "Because it didn't last very long. Besides, right after it happened, your grandpa..." He trailed off, trying to think of the best phrasing to use, but Ryan nodded in understanding. "It was a while back," Willy went on. "No big deal. I'm over it."

"A few weeks," Chyann repeated, bewildered.

Willy waved his hands. "All right all right, can we get back on topic, please?" Chyann and Ryan shared a knowing look, then sat back down.

Ryan shoved aside a pile of old books on Chyann's desk. "Well, I read some stuff about hellhounds that could be helpful. Also found a list of a few things we might be able to dig up that can deal with it."

"Are we even sure that's what it is?" Chyann asked. "We didn't get a chance to look for omens, but Linda mentioned a bad smell lingering around the house before her mom died."

Ryan gently rubbed the side of his head, squinting his eyes in pain. "It's not much, but it doesn't rule out hellhounds. According to the lore and the passages about demons in my grandpa's journal, hellhounds are like the debt collectors for deals with demons, among other things. Usually people can get whatever they want out of the deal–success, talent, or even love. I figure she made a deal with some demon, couldn't pay her debt, and had to fork her soul over for it."

"If that's the case, then we're done here, right?" Willy replied. "The thing turned Shawntell into a chew toy and went back to hell or whatever. Don't you think?"

Ryan clamped his eyes shut. He seemed to really be hurting. "Yeah, I dunno. Maybe."

Chyann stood and went to her bathroom. A moment later she returned with a glass of water and a bottle of aspirin. She handed them to Ryan and plopped back down.

"Thanks." He grabbed a few pills, gulped them down, and continued, "It sucks to say, but there isn't anything else we can do unless the whole family made a deal with a demon. Will's right. We're done here."

"Well, then I've got a puppy to catch," Willy said. "It popped up right before Shawntell bit the big one. Maybe it had something to do with this?"

Ryan nodded. "We should probably pick up the stuff used to hold off hellhounds, too. Even if the problem resolved itself, it'd be nice to have more gear on hand."

Willy climbed to his feet. "Fine. You two get some hoodoo to send this thing to a kennel, and I'll catch the puppy."

"You sure you don't just want an excuse to see your girlfriend again?" Chyann teased, smirking.

Willy headed toward the door. "Bite me."

"Don't do anything we wouldn't do!" Chyann called after him.

Rolling his eyes, Willy exited the room and started down the stairs. *If she ever has another crush, I'm tellin' that guy to steer clear.*

WILLY WANDERED DOWN THE HOSPITAL HALLWAY toward AJ's room. He'd intended to head over to the Blake house to find that puppy, but he took a last minute bus here instead. *AJ was always a cool kid*, he thought, and the desire to visit the young boy was too strong to turn down.

Truth be told, though, Willy wasn't sure why he wanted to visit AJ in the first place. He hadn't spoken to the kid, or to Linda, in over a year. Why did he care so much now?

It wasn't as if he and Linda had stayed friends after things ended. They'd just… broken up. That was it.

He rounded a corner, his wet sneakers squeaking against the floor. It was dark outside due to the weather and time of day. Rain pattered against the glass windows around him.

He stopped at the third room down the hall. According to the receptionist he'd spoken to, this was where AJ was staying: room 503.

Willy hovered near the entrance. *Do I knock? Or just go in? Would he care that I came to see him? Would Linda?*

"Willy?" the familiar voice of a girl said from behind him. He flinched and swung around. Linda had appeared from around the corner. "What are you doing here?" she asked.

Willy glanced at AJ's door before facing her. He forced a smile. "I'm, uhh, y'know. You said AJ was here, so I thought I'd come check on him."

Linda crossed her arms and shifted her weight to one leg. "He and my dad are sleeping right now. He's going home tomorrow night."

Willy stuffed his hands into his sweater pocket.

"Gotcha. I'll, uhh…" He stepped past her to leave. "I'll just drop by some other time."

"Why did you come in the first place?"

Willy paused. "Like I said, to see AJ." He swung around to look at her.

She shook her head, her black hair moving side to side. "The last time we talked was just over a year ago. You said we might as well act like we'd never met. Now I've seen you twice in one day?" She stepped closer. "What's up with that?"

Willy forced a laugh. "You're right. I shouldn't have swung by."

He turned to leave again, but Linda grabbed his wrist and pulled him back. "No, I wanna know what's going on." There was a stern tone in her voice, a harsh expression on her face.

Willy stayed silent. *The hell am I supposed to tell her?*

Linda's expression softened a bit, some of the anger fading from her voice as she spoke. "Are your parents fighting again or something?"

He chuckled. "They're *always* fighting."

She released him. "Did it get worse?"

"Does it matter?"

She lowered her arm and began scratching it. "It does to me."

Willy couldn't help but roll his eyes. "Sure it does."

"Hey, what's *that* supposed to mean?"

Willy paused. "Forget it."

Linda scratched herself furiously. "Just because we broke up doesn't mean I stopped caring. You wouldn't be here now if you didn't still care, too."

He went quiet. Maybe she was right. Despite everything that had happened between them, it *was* nice to see her again. He just hated the pain that came with it.

He glanced at her arm. Linda sighed in frustration and sat down on a bench, focusing entirely on scratching what must have been raw skin by this point.

Willy pointed at her arm. "You got fleas or somethin'?"

Linda scowled. "A rash. And a super-weird, stubborn one at that."

"Weird how?"

She pulled her sleeve up and showed him her forearm. The skin was pink and red, though he couldn't be sure whether the discoloration was from her constant scratching or the rash itself. However, what caught his attention more than anything else was the arrangement of hives dotting her skin.

He leaned closer to inspect it. "It's shaped almost like a bite."

"Nothing bit me, though," she said. "The doctors haven't seen anything like it. It doesn't respond to ice or itch cream, either. It's driving me insane."

Willy shot upright and stuffed his hands into his pockets. "You seen or heard anything strange lately?"

Linda furrowed her brow and resumed her scratching. "Like what?"

"Humor me."

She paused before looking down at the floor. "I don't think I got it because of anything strange… I'm pretty sure I got it from my mom." She turned to him again. "She had one just like it before she…"

Willy mulled over her words for a bit. *Is it just a rash? Or could it be something else?*

"Anyway," Linda continued, "my Dad has one too. AJ'll probably catch it, considering how much we've been around him the last few days." She narrowed her eyes in suspicion at Willy. "What's wrong?"

Shit, I probably look freaked. He forced another smile. "Nothin'. Just wish you would'a led with that so I could'a kept a safe distance." He swung around and hurried off. "I gotta go!"

"Willy, wait!" Linda called after him, but he didn't wait, didn't even look back.

He had another stop to make before meeting up with Ryan and Chyann again.

A STREETLIGHT OVERHEAD HUMMED AS CHYANN climbed out of her car. She pulled her hood over her hair and turned to Ryan. He closed the passenger door, then tugged his hood up as well. "You ready?" he asked.

Chyann stared past him at the familiar iron barrier surrounding Heaven's Gate Cemetery. Memories of the night she'd helped the boys dig up and burn the body of Adella Williams surfaced in her thoughts. "I guess so," she responded, walking around her car to follow him across the street.

Once they reached the gate, Ryan handed Chyann the small shovel he'd brought and began climbing over. "Be careful," Chyann said.

"Relax," Ryan reassured her. "It's not like I haven't done this before."

Soon he reached the other side and dropped to the grass, safe and sound. Chyann handed him the shovel through the bars, then climbed up and over herself.

As she jumped down onto the wet lawn, Ryan started into the cemetery. The pouring rain created a thin mist that swirled around the gravestones. Chyann hugged her sides and followed Ryan. "So, uhh, what are we doing out here again?"

He pulled a small empty jar from his jacket pocket. "I read in my grandpa's journal that graveyard dirt is a good way to keep hellhounds off you. It's supposed to be like salt against spirits."

"That kinda makes sense, actually," Chyann said. "Most cemeteries are consecrated ground. In the mythology, holy stuff usually deters things that come from hell."

Ryan gave her a sideways grin. "Somebody's been doing their homework."

Chyann grinned back. "*Somebody's* gotta keep your ass alive."

After some more walking, Ryan stopped under a tree that blocked them from the worst of the storm. "Right here should be good."

They knelt, and Ryan handed the jar to Chyann. She opened it and held it out for him to fill. He dug through the mud, taking small clumps without grass and carefully dumping them into the jar.

Chyann looked around to make sure nobody else happened to be out in the storm. "So, Willy and Linda, huh?"

"I know. Super wild. Never took Willy for the 'relationship' type."

"Why do you think he never told us about it?"

Ryan shrugged. "Dunno. Normally he's pretty kiss-and-tell. Whatever happened between them must have been kinda serious if he kept it from us."

Chyann nodded. Willy was notorious for getting into day-or-two-long flings with girls around school. He loved to brag about them when he did, too, much to Chyann's dismay. She usually couldn't get him to shut up about stuff like this, so the deal with Linda was weird.

Ryan finished filling the jar, set the shovel down, and took the container from Chyann. Then he popped the lid on and rose to his feet.

Chyann stood as well. "Do you think she broke his heart?"

Ryan thought for a second. "Maybe, yeah. He was really persistent about it *not* being a big deal. And you know how Will is when it comes to touchy-feely situations."

"She must have really hurt him…"

Awkward silence settled between the two of them.

Eventually, Ryan raised the jar. "This should be enough for now. Let's head back and see if Will caught that puppy yet." He moved past her.

She turned and followed Ryan to leave. "Should we ask him about it? About Linda?"

"Probably not," Ryan answered. "He might be all mixed-up right now. He'll tell us more when he's ready."

She sighed. "Yeah, probably. I just wish I knew what happened." She had fun teasing Willy, especially because he never settled on one girl for long. Honestly, it was a shock to hear he had at one time. But the more she thought about it, the more concerned she became.

What did Linda do to make him keep this from us for so long?

ILLY EXITED SHAWNTELL'S ART STUDIO AND closed the door. *Nothing in there, either.*

He'd once again picked his way into the house now that he knew no one would be there, and he'd spent the last fifteen minutes searching the place for omens. So far, there hadn't been any. No dead plants, no bad smells, nothing. The house was clean.

Is it really a hellhound? he wondered.

He knew that it burned paw prints into the floor. He also knew that it left marks on people. So if it wasn't a hellhound, what could it be?

One thing was for sure: this problem wasn't yet resolved.

Willy walked down the hall toward the back door. As he passed one of the windows, he glanced outside and spotted a dark shape by the doghouse. He paused, trying to make out what it was through the rain running down the glass.

Oh, it's the puppy. The little guy sniffed around the doghouse, then trotted into the structure, shook itself off, and curled up on the wood, shivering. *Poor thing.*

Willy opened the back door, stepped outside, and locked up the house before venturing farther into the cold. He hopped off the porch and moved toward the doghouse.

The puppy's ears perked up. It lifted its head as Willy approached.

Willy crouched down. "Hey, little dude."

The puppy eyed him suspiciously, still shivering.

"Havin' a hard time stayin' warm and dry nowadays, huh?" The closer Willy looked, the more he noticed how thin the thing was. "Not doin' so good on food, either."

The puppy huffed, its ears going flat against its head.

"Well, I'll tell you what. I know a place that's warm, dry, and probably has somethin' you can eat." He stuck his hand into the doghouse for the puppy to smell.

The animal gave the tips of his fingers a half-hearted sniff. A whole minute passed before it decided Willy was trustworthy. It staggered to its feet and took a few uneasy steps toward him.

Willy gently lifted the puppy into his arms. He cradled it, shielding it from the rain as best he could. "There ya go, bud. Let's get outta this crap before we both freeze to death, huh?"

The puppy whined and rested its head against Willy's chest. With the puppy secured, he hastened out of the yard and ran to Chyann's house.

CHAPTER 4

THE PUPPY BARKED AS WILLY WIPED him off with a towel; it had become a regular motion for Willy since he brought the dog home last night.

Chyann wheeled around in her desk chair. "Why is he so loud?"

Willy plopped down onto a beanbag and let the puppy go. "He's a puppy, Chy. Puppies are loud."

The puppy ran around the bedroom, stopping only to sniff something before bounding toward another corner.

Ryan sat on Chyann's bed. The boy lowered a hand to pet the dog as he raced by. "He'll probably quiet down when he gets older."

Chyann turned back to her computer. "You say that like we're gonna keep him."

The dog collided with Chyann's bookshelf, too busy sniffing the floor to watch where he was going. Willy grinned. *This little doofus*, he thought, and faced Chyann. "Who says we aren't?"

"Me," Chyann said sternly. "At least not in my room."

"You should be glad he's already housebroken," Willy replied.

Chyann shook her head as she continued scrolling through pages on her computer screen. "Man, I'm one lucky girl."

Willy snorted, and the puppy strolled up next to him and flopped down against his leg. Willy scratched him behind the ear. "She's just mad 'cause I let you chew on her shoes while she was asleep last night."

Chyann whirled around, eyes wide. "You *what*?"

Willy brought a hand to his mouth. "Oh jeez, that was supposed to be a secret." He winked at her. "Anyway, like I was sayin', I went through the whole place top to bottom, and I didn't see any omens."

Ryan took his grandpa's journal off Chyann's desk and threw it open. "Maybe we missed something."

There was a sudden flash of light as Boss appeared over the left side of Ryan's face. "Perhaps you–"

The puppy jolted to his feet and barked at the Ooawan. Willy patted the pooch on the back and pulled him into his lap. "Easy, dude. He's one of the good guys." The puppy stopped barking, but he growled a few times.

"Apologies," Boss said in a low voice. "I should have given more of a warning."

Ryan cleared his throat. "You were saying?"

Willy furrowed his brow. *What the hell was that?* Ryan seemed... irritated, now that Boss was here. Was he fighting with Boss or something?

Boss gave the puppy a sideways glance before focusing on the journal. "Perhaps you were on the right track, but looking at the wrong culprit."

"What do you mean?" Chyann asked. "Are you suggesting it isn't a hellhound, but some other dog-creature?"

"Precisely."

Willy scratched his cheek, thoughts of Ryan and Boss quickly replaced by the memory of Linda's strange rash. "Anything in that old journal say somethin' about a creature that leaves marks on people?"

Ryan and Chyann turned to him, curious expressions on their faces. "Marks?" Ryan asked. "What kind of marks?"

Willy gestured at Chyann. "When we saw Linda, she kept scratching her arm, remember?"

"I remember, yeah, but we didn't see why. She was wearing a sweater. Unless…" Chyann sat for a moment before pointing an accusatory finger at Willy. "You went and saw her again, didnt you?"

Willy rolled his eyes. "Oh, brother…"

Chyann laughed. "You did!"

Willy pointed at his forearm. "She had a rash that looked like a *bite* on her arm."

Ryan knit his brow. "A rash that looked like a bite?"

"Yeah," Willy answered. "And she said her mom came down with one just like it right before she died." Ryan began frantically flipping through the journal's many pages.

Chyann remained focused on Willy. "Why'd you go back?"

Willy groaned. "I didn't. I happened to run into her again, all right? Stop askin.'"

"It's just weird, Will," Chyann said. "First we find out you were with a girl longer than a day, and then you start acting like it's no big deal."

"Because it isn't a big deal!"

"Then why didn't you tell us?"

Willy shook his head and climbed to his feet. Tears burned in his eyes, threatening to rise to the surface, but he wasn't about to cry over this. Especially not in front of Ryan and Chyann. "I need some air."

He stormed out of the bedroom, and on his way to the ground floor, he skipped steps. Rather than going through the front door ahead on the right, he went left, crossed the living room, and headed toward the patio in the backyard. He slid the back door open, stepped outside, and stopped at the edge of the short porch.

The air was cold, and the wind didn't help the temperature, but the roof and the rest of the house shielded him from the rain, thankfully.

He sat down and stared out at the downpour. Why couldn't Chyann and Ryan just drop the thing about Linda? What happened with her was old news. Done and over with, and from so long ago. Why did it matter now? There was no sense in bringing it up. Especially now, when there was a monster out killing people, and they still weren't sure how to stop it.

Something wet touched his hand. He looked down to see the puppy. The little guy gave his hand a few licks before scurrying into the yard. *Must've followed me down here.*

The dog made a quick lap around the yard before coming back and curling up in Willy's lap.

He ran a hand down the puppy's back a few times, then gave his head a gentle pat. "At least *someone* around here isn't grilling me about ex-girlfriends."

The puppy shook his head, water droplets splattering across Willy's face. He chuckled. "Thanks for the shower, ya prick." The dog panted, staring up at Willy as he continued petting him. "I bet you'd be one hell of a guard dog when you're bigger. With that loud-ass yipe you got, everybody in a three-block radius would…"

A thought struck Willy. *Davey. That big dog back at the Flecks' house.* After defeating Woody, the trio had briefly discussed how Davey acted strangely whenever he'd been around the dummy.

Willy stared into the puppy's deep-brown eyes. "Son of a bitch." He lifted the animal out of his lap and jumped to his feet. "C'mon, little guy!"

He sprinted back into the house, heading for the stairs. The puppy's claws scratched against the floor as he scrambled after Willy.

Willy shot up the stairs and halted in the doorway. "Guys, we gotta get back to the Blakes."

Chyann, Ryan, and Boss shared looks of concern. "Why?" Chyann asked.

"Remember Davey? He got wigged-out whenever Woody was around."

"Right," Ryan said. "Dogs are usually more sensitive to the supernatural."

The puppy shoved himself between Willy's legs. Willy motioned at the animal. "So, what if this little dude was hangin' around the house 'cause he was tryin' to *warn them* about whatever attacked Shawntell?"

Boss hummed. "It's possible, I suppose. It would explain why the creature went near the house so often."

Ryan swung his legs off the bed and set his grandpa's journal down. "Well, nobody's there now, right?"

Willy's stomach dropped as he recalled his conversation with Linda. "Linda said they're bringing AJ home tonight. Maybe they're there, gettin' things ready."

Ryan and Chyann stood and threw their jackets on. Chyann pulled her car keys out of her pocket. "Let's go."

Willy nodded before turning and heading back down the stairs. He whistled at the puppy. "Let's go, ya little doofus."

The dog heeded the call and followed him to the front door.

I hope we're not too late.

L INDA FOLLOWED HER FATHER INTO THEIR HOME. She closed the door behind herself and headed for the stairs. "I'll get his room ready."

"Linda," Dad said from behind her. She stopped halfway up the stairs and turned to look down at him. His expression was soft but stern. He made eye contact with her and didn't break it as he continued. "We're going to sit down and have a serious talk after AJ is in bed tonight."

Her chest tightened. She had known this was coming. She just wished it didn't have to. There was no escaping it, though. She'd have to face it eventually.

Her bottom lip quivered, and she lowered her head and nodded.

"All right," he said quietly. "Go ahead and close his curtains. Unplug his game consoles, too. Staring at a television playing games is the last thing he needs right now." He scratched his arm. Linda's own arm twitched every now and again, mostly when the burning got really bad. "I'll make sure the house is secure in case whatever attacked your mom is still in the neighborhood."

"Did animal control tell you anything yet?"

Dad sighed in frustration. "No. As far as I know, they haven't found a damn thing."

Linda couldn't stop herself from scratching her arm through her jacket. "Hopefully soon."

"Yeah, hopefully." He trudged into the kitchen.

Linda finished going up the stairs and started down the hallway. Halfway down on the left was AJ's room. She opened the door.

It was as messy as ever, with dirty clothes on the floor, an unmade bed in the corner, and empty water bottles and soda cans covering the desk next to the bed.

A wireless game controller lay on AJ's pillow, which Linda knew was connected to the console on his TV stand to her right. *I better start with that before I make the room too dark.*

As she began unplugging wires and pulling the console out of place, a familiar sound made its way to her ears. *Is that the puppy Willy said was his?*

She strode across the bedroom to peer out the window into the backyard. The puppy was there, but so were Willy, Chyann Wakeman, and Ryan Myers. They stood in the yard, staring at the house and talking as the puppy barked.

What the hell are they doing here? This was the third time she'd seen Willy in two days. Was he following her?

She'd heard the rumors about Ryan, about how he was some sort of cultist, and the way Willy had been acting last night at the hospital still weighed on her mind. Something was going on, and whatever it was, it couldn't be good.

Her palms grew sweaty. *I don't know what they want, but I gotta get them out of here.*

She pulled her cell phone from her pocket and raced out of the room, then hurried down the steps and ran to the back door.

Her father stopped what he was doing and stepped aside to let her by. "What's wrong?"

"Somebody's in the backyard," she answered, bounding out the door.

When Willy saw her, he let out a long sigh. He almost seemed... relieved. "Linda, you're okay."

"You need to leave," she snapped. "I don't know what you're doing here, but I don't wanna talk."

Willy raised his hands in defense, and the puppy kept barking. "Hear me out."

Dad stepped up next to her on the porch. "What's going on out here?" He narrowed his eyes at Willy. "Wait, I know you."

"Leave, now," Linda repeated, raising her cell phone. "Leave, or I call the cops."

"Just give me a sec to explain, okay?"

She shook her head. "You had your chance to talk to me last night."

"It wasn't a wild animal that killed your mom!" Willy shouted. "It was something else, and it might still be around here."

"Listen to him, Linda," Chyann piped up.

Willy opened his mouth to say something else, but Dad stomped forward. "She said to leave, kid. She's serious about calling the police. Take that dog, and get the hell off my lawn."

Willy balled his fists. "I'll get off your lawn when–"

"Will, stop," Ryan said, grabbing him by the shoulder. "We need to leave."

Willy spun around to face Ryan. "Dude."

Ryan glanced up at Linda and her father. He whispered something to Willy, but Linda couldn't hear what.

Willy's expression grew solemn. Linda raised her eyebrows at him. She'd never seen this side of him before. They'd had serious talks when they'd been together, sure, but he'd always acted too relaxed. He'd been calm, cracking jokes. This was different. His face was… grim.

Without speaking, Willy scooped up the still-barking dog. He looked straight at Linda before following Ryan and Chyann into the alleyway and out of sight.

Once they were gone, Dad turned to her. "What was that all about?" Concern laced his voice. "Didn't you date that kid a while back?"

Linda nodded. "Yeah, for a little while."

"What was that nonsense he said about your mother?"

"I don't know. He keeps popping up since Mom died. He's acting really weird. I just… saw them out here and got scared. I don't know what's going on."

He patted her shoulder. "Take a breath, honey. We'll figure it out. Come on, let's head back in." He guided her to the door, and she stepped back into the warm house.

Once she was inside, the rash on her arm began burning worse than ever before.

She fought the urge to scratch it. Her dad shut the door behind them.

Just as he locked it, a foul smell invaded her nostrils.

WILLY PLODDED THROUGH PUDDLE AFTER PUDDLE with the puppy squirming in his grip. Thankfully, the little dude had stopped barking a few minutes ago.

They all exited the alleyway, Chyann's car just up ahead. *What's gonna happen to Linda now?* he wondered, swallowing hard.

Rain pelted his body, but he hardly noticed. All he could think about were worst-case scenarios in which some monster was tearing through Linda. Worst-case scenarios in which he couldn't save her.

Chyann walked ahead of him and Ryan. "So what now? Are we just leaving?"

Ryan gestured back at the house. "Well, we can't go back. Not unless we want the cops breathing down our necks."

"We don't even know what we're dealing with," Chyann said. "What if it attacks again?"

Willy set the puppy down. "We're not talkin' about killing it, Chy. We're talkin' about keepin' it from icing Linda."

"How?" Chyann asked. "It could be a bear for all we know."

The puppy barked once, loudly, catching all of them by surprise. Willy glanced down at the dog. He stood alert, facing the direction of the Blake home. He gazed up at Willy, and something in his eyes told Willy all he needed to know.

With another bark, the puppy sprinted off down the alley. Willy shared looks with Chyann and Ryan. No one said anything, but they knew what had to be done.

Together, they hurried back toward the house.

*L*INDA COVERED HER NOSE AND MOUTH WITH HER sleeve to block out the putrid scent. She gagged before choking out, "What *is* that?"

Dad knelt next to her. He looked like he was about to vomit. "I don't know."

A dark shape suddenly appeared, slamming into them. Linda flew backward. She rammed into a wall and fell sideways to the floor. Screams pierced the air– her dad's screams.

Pain arced up and down her arm from where her elbow made contact with the floor. She forced her eyes open.

Whatever hit her had knocked her into the kitchen. She looked up, saw the kitchen counter. *I must have slammed into it.* She gazed into the hall but saw nothing. No sign of her dad, though she could hear him howling in pain.

There was a wet ripping noise. His yells stopped.

Linda's breath caught in her throat. She tried hoisting herself to her feet, but she didn't have the strength. The burning on her arm was unbearable, as if a colony of fire ants were tearing through her flesh with their mandibles.

A growl echoed through the room. What Linda saw next almost made her heart stop.

Smoke rose from the floor in swirling tendrils, creeping toward her. As the smoke neared, Linda realized that paw prints were appearing, *burning* themselves into the wood, as something unseen inched toward her.

Two smoldering crimson orbs that looked like eyes materialized from behind the smoke. The head they must belong to took shape as well. Whatever this creature was, it seemed to be some kind of canine.

Her suspicions were confirmed as a large dog emerged from the smoke, baring its fangs. Its fur was so dark it appeared as though it had no color at all–like an endless black void. Drool dripped from its maw down to the floor, its paws singeing the wood with every step, its glowing red eyes filled with hate. Despite how clearly Linda could see the beast, she had no idea what breed it was. In fact, it didn't appear to have a breed at all. It was just generically dog-shaped.

She tried to scream, but the horrid stench in the air caused her to gag again. She couldn't stand, couldn't yell, couldn't get away. *I'm gonna die!*

The black dog hovered over her, standing nearly four feet tall even on all fours. Its hot breath grazed her face, another growl sounding from the back of its throat.

The back door swung open. Willy ran into the house, shovel in hand. Ryan and Chyann followed close behind him.

The black dog spun around to face the teenagers. As they looked at the creature, they stopped in their tracks.

Willy was first to move. He raised the shovel high and charged at the creature. "Back off, Fido!" He swung the tool, batting the hound to the side with a resounding *ping*.

The dog yiped, stumbling back, and vanished from sight.

Willy offered a hand to Linda. "You hurt?" She grabbed his wrist, and he helped her stand.

Her mind raced with questions. She gave herself a once-over. "I–I don't think so."

Ryan scanned the room. "Where did that thing go?"

Linda moved closer to Willy as he turned back to his friends. He raised the shovel again. "I don't know, but let's not stick around and find out."

Willy, Ryan, and Chyann started for the door, but Linda didn't move with them. "Wait, my dad!" she shouted. She turned to peer down the hall and caught sight of something wet on the floor. As she stepped closer, her stomach churned.

There was a hand–a *bloody* hand–severed from its body, unmoving in a pool of crimson.

Linda stopped dead. It couldn't be–

Someone grabbed her arm. She turned to see it was Willy. He gave her a serious look and lowered the shovel. "We'll figure this out later, okay? But right now we gotta bail."

Linda tried to reply but found she couldn't speak. Her voice was gone.

Willy tugged her arm, dragging her along as he sprinted out the back door. Soon they caught up with Ryan and Chyann, the little black puppy barking as they approached. When Ryan and Chyann ran through the open gate, the puppy spun and followed them out of the backyard.

Before she knew it, Linda was in the alleyway behind her home. A vicious growl sounded in the air, and she stopped to look back.

Willy stepped in front of her protectively. Together, the four teens gazed at the back door of the house.

The demonic black dog hovered in the doorway, glaring at them. It raised its head and howled, smoke billowing out from under it, then disappeared from sight.

Almost instantly, the burning of the rash on Linda's arm faded ever so slightly.

For now, it seemed the beast was gone.

CHAPTER 5

THE SCENT OF LARRY'S DINER ALWAYS made Willy hungry–even during dire situations. Larry fixed a mean burger, obviously, and that made it a popular menu item. Between the aromas of the sandwiches he was constantly cooking, and the ones people were constantly eating, the air was filled with the most delicious of smells.

The puppy must have felt the same as Willy, because he sat under the table, pouting as Willy and his friends waited for their meals. "I know, dude. Don't worry. Food is on the way," Willy said. The puppy whined and rested his head on Willy's foot.

Willy looked up at the others sitting at the booth with him. Ryan and Chyann were across from him.

Ryan read through his grandpa's journal, while Chyann sat with her hands clasped. Linda was next to Willy, staring out the window in silence.

Linda's eyes were red and puffy, her hair wet and matted because of their run from Linda's house to Chyann's car. Once they'd reached the vehicle, they'd driven back to Chyann's place, then gone to Larry's. Despite the day she was having, Linda still looked super pretty.

"A Black Dog?" Chyann asked Ryan.

Ryan set down the journal and slid it over to Willy so he could read it. "A Black Dog," Ryan confirmed.

Willy skimmed the pages and saw a rough sketch of a canine creature with red eyes. Many other images were paper clipped to the pages—ones featuring more Black Dogs. There was even a photo of claw marks burnt into an old wood door.

"According to my grandpa's entries," Ryan started, "Black Dogs are the spirits of man's best friend who come back to take revenge on their *owners* for causing their deaths."

Fresh terror washed over Linda's face as she looked down at the journal alongside Willy.

Ryan pointed at her. "That bite on your arm is the dog's way of marking you for death. Whatever happened, his spirit blames you. And your mom, and your dad, and maybe even your brother."

Linda trembled all over, staring down at the pictures as if in a trance. Willy reached out and took her hand. She glanced at him and swallowed hard.

Willy gave her hand a squeeze. "What happened?"

Linda squirmed in her seat. She took a shaky breath before speaking. "Three days ago, I went out driving after school. It had just started raining when I left, and it had gotten pretty bad by the time I was on my way home. I wasn't speeding, but I wasn't driving slow, either. I–I–I looked away from the road for one second to check something on my phone, and then..." Tears streamed down her cheeks, and she wiped her face with her free hand. "Next thing I know, AJ and Buddy are on the ground in front of my car. I guess they were crossing the street and I didn't see them. AJ got clipped by the corner, but Buddy..."

She fell quiet, struggling to hold back her tears, and Willy's chest grew tight. Ryan and Chyann offered her sorrowful looks.

"What were they doin' out in the rain, anyway?" Willy asked.

Linda sniffed. "I guess AJ had a pretty nasty fight with my dad while I was out, and AJ took Buddy with him to get away." She grabbed a napkin off the table and dabbed her eyes with it. "The accident wasn't far from my house, so my parents showed up fast. My dad drove me and AJ to the hospital, and my mom was supposed to take Buddy to the vet, but Buddy didn't last..." She blew her nose into the napkin before setting it on the table. "Later that night, she told my dad she *let* Buddy die."

Willy smiled awkwardly at Chyann and Ryan, whose expressions were twisted with disgust and horror. "Did I mention Shawntell hated dogs?" He cleared his throat. "So, if this thing is a ghost, how come I managed to clobber it with a shovel earlier?"

Ryan pulled the journal back and flipped through the pages. "According to the entry and a couple of Grandpa's books back home, spirits generate this sticky black goo called ectoplasm. The angrier the spirit, the more ectoplasm they make." He stopped on a page marked *SPIRITS* in big bold letters and turned it around for Willy to see. "If they're mean enough, some ghosts can even become solid figures made of the stuff when they manifest."

Willy nodded. "So he's gotta be one seriously pissed-off pooch."

"I can't believe this is happening," Linda mumbled.

"Hey," Willy started, trying to be reassuring, "this is *good* news." Linda gave him a confused look. He grinned. "We already know how to give a ghost the boot."

Linda finally squeezed his hand back and offered a weak smile. She lifted her free hand and scratched her arm again before facing Ryan with a panicked look in her eyes. "Oh, God–AJ. He's all by himself at the hospital."

"Does he have a rash too?" Ryan asked.

"I have no idea."

Chyann and Ryan climbed out of the booth. Ryan rubbed his left eye and winced. "We better check on him, then. Chy can go back to the hospital with you. Will, you and I need to grab some gear before we meet back up."

"You want me to protect them all by myself?" Chyann asked. "What if the Black Dog shows up?"

Ryan clamped his eyes shut. "Grab some salt from the cafeteria once you get there. A ghost is a ghost. Salt should still work. Not as well as rock salt, but it'll buy you time until Will and I get there with the good stuff."

Willy scooted out of the booth next. "What about our food?"

Chyann put her hands on her hips. "Get it to-go."

There was a whine below Willy, and he looked down to see the puppy begging with sad eyes once again. Willy looked back to Chyann and pointed at the dog. "Great, Chy. Now you made him sad."

Chyann rolled her eyes and turned to Linda. "Are you ready to go?"

"Yeah." Linda wiped her face with her sleeve.

"I'll go start the car." With that, Chyann exited the diner.

Linda crossed her arms and turned to Willy. "What's gonna happen?"

Willy glanced at Ryan. The other boy was pressing his palms against his head, his eyes shut tight. "If everything goes well," Willy said, "you'll be rash free. After that… I dunno."

"Is this just what you guys do? Stop ghosts and things?"

Willy smirked. "Yeah, we're kinda pros at it." She didn't return his jest, so he opted for a more serious tone. "We've done this a couple times. I won't let anything happen to ya."

"Promise?"

Willy raised his arms in defense. "C'mon, Lin, this is *me* we're talkin' about."

Linda didn't answer, but she did give him the smallest of smiles before turning around and following Chyann out of the diner.

Willy dropped his arms to his sides. Ryan grunted, digging his nails into his palms. "You ready?"

Willy gestured at the puppy. "Yeah, just lemme go get our food so this little guy stops whinin' at me."

The dog barked once and followed Willy toward the front counter. *I gotta get this done, no matter what. For her.*

CHYANN FOLLOWED LINDA THROUGH THE HOSPI-
tal toward AJ's room. Initially, she'd been worried
about running into her mom or Ryan's mom while she
was here, but thankfully, AJ's room was on a different
floor than the one they normally worked.

Before the girls had headed up to AJ's room, they'd
made a quick stop in the cafeteria to find some salt.
There had been a half-full can on the counter next to
the food line, which Chyann had taken when nobody
was looking. She patted her jacket pocket to ensure it
hadn't fallen out.

Once they reached the room, Linda knocked twice
and opened the door. Chyann followed her inside,
then closed up behind them.

The room was dim. AJ lay in bed, his black hair
peeking out from underneath clean wrappings. He
seemed relieved at the sight of Linda, but when he
spotted Chyann, his eyes went wide with curiosity.

"Are you okay?" Linda asked, sitting on the bed
next to him.

AJ glanced between her and Chyann. "I–I'm fine,
sis. What's going on? Who's this? Where's Dad?"

Linda took his hand in hers. "Dad is… When we
went home, the creature that attacked Mom was there."

Despite the lighting, Chyann saw the color drain
from AJ's face.

Linda gave him a moment to process her words
before she continued. "This is Chyann. She and her

friends saved me before the thing could get me, too. They're going to help us stop it."

AJ shook his head a few times. "What is it? Some kind of wolf?" His voice held a tremor.

She's being pretty vague with him here, Chyann thought. *But it's more than that. Does he know she was the one who hit him and Buddy?*

Linda patted his hand. "Something like that, yeah. We're gonna stop it before it hurts anyone else, all right?"

AJ opened his mouth to respond but stopped. He resorted to nodding and turning away. Chyann saw his expression twist in agony, and tears began streaming down his cheeks.

Linda sat silently next to him. Chyann's chest tightened as she watched them. Immense tragedy had befallen their family, and she couldn't begin to imagine how they felt.

"I'll be outside," Chyann whispered. She stepped back and opened the door wide enough to slip out. But before she left the room, she glanced at AJ's arm.

There was no rash. The Black Dog hadn't marked him.

At least, not yet.

RYAN'S GARAGE DOOR OPENED, AND WILLY SCURried inside to escape the rain. Between how much it was coming down, and how often he was out in it, he had begun to think he'd never be dry again.

The puppy squeezed between Willy's and Ryan's legs and shook himself off. Ryan closed the door behind them and flicked on the light overhead. "Home sweet home." He moved past Willy to the door that led into the basement and began his descent. Willy followed, watching his feet as the puppy trotted next to him.

Ryan turned on a light as they went down. "So, what're we gonna do with the puppy when we're done?"

The dog ran ahead and sniffed around. Willy shrugged. "Dunno. When we get Linda and AJ outta this, maybe they can take him."

They entered what had once been Magnus's room, and Ryan hauled the trunk out of the closet while Willy grabbed the duffel bag out from under the bed. They picked up gear from the trunk and tossed it into the bag. "Stay with Linda if you want," Ryan said. "Chy and I can take care of this."

"You kiddin' me?" Willy laughed. "I'm gonna *Old Yeller* this bastard. End of discussion." The puppy popped up next to him and sniffed the stuff in his hands. "Not you, pal."

"I'm just tossing the idea out there," Ryan replied. "It's pretty obvious you still like her."

Willy sighed. "You two ever gonna give it a rest?"

Ryan chuckled. "Sorry, sorry. It's just wild to us that you never said anything."

"Yeah, well..." Willy paused, patting the puppy on the head. "That's because there was nothin' worth talkin' about."

Ryan set a can of rock salt in the bag and zipped it shut. "What happened?"

Willy sat down on the bed. The puppy climbed into his lap and curled up with a big yawn. He smiled and gave the little guy a few more scratches.

It was better to think about the puppy instead of Linda. Willy didn't like to remember the night they'd broken up, or how drastically his world had shifted because of it. "We just didn't work," he mumbled.

Ryan pursed his lips. Willy wasn't sure whether Ryan believed him, but the other boy didn't press further. Instead, he threw the duffel bag over his shoulder. "Well, let's go to the girls. We've got business to take care of."

Willy lifted the puppy into his arms and followed Ryan out of the room. Ryan turned off the lights, and they started up the stairs.

The dog gazed up to Willy with half-open eyes. *He must be tired,* Willy thought. *He's been following us around all day.* He stroked the dog's cheek.

When they reached the top of the stairs, Willy asked, "You got a few blankets I can stuff him in? He's probably had enough of the rain."

Ryan set the duffel bag down next to the garage door and headed into the house. "Yeah, sure. Hold on."

"Thanks."

Ryan shut the door behind him, leaving Willy and the puppy alone in the garage. Willy looked over at the workbench to his left and saw a handful of large iron nails scattered atop it. *If only there was a nail gun big enough to shoot those babies.*

He glanced at the door leading into the backyard. Pushed against the wall next to it was a crutch, an old cane, and a thick wooden baseball bat.

He smirked and set the puppy down. The dog whined at him. "I know, dude. Just trust me." Scanning the wall above the workbench, he spotted a hammer. He snatched the tool. "I've got an idea."

THE HOSPITAL HALL WAS A BIT TOO CHILLY FOR Chyann. She sat on the bench across from AJ's room, her hands stuffed in her jacket pockets.

Rain pelted the window to her left, thunder roaring in the distance. She wondered whether the storm would worsen. *I hope the boys make it here okay...*

There was a *squeak*, and Chyann looked over to see Linda exit AJ's room. Linda closed the door behind herself and leaned against the wall. She slid down to the floor, letting out a long breath. "He's sleeping while we wait."

Chyann rested her elbows on her knees. "Linda, I'm sorry."

"For what?"

"For everything that's happened to you and AJ. No matter what, neither of you deserve this."

Linda scratched her arm. "Yeah... I don't know. It seems like Buddy thinks so."

Chyann took a deep breath but said nothing.

"My mom was always kinda hard to figure out, you know?" Linda went on. She rolled up her sleeve. "She acted like all she ever cared about was her work. She could be pretty cold to me and AJ sometimes, but I think it was her way of keeping us tough."

Chyann nodded, thoughts of her own mother springing to mind. "I can understand that."

"I had this teacher back in elementary. She *hated* me. I probably misbehaved, but not any more than the other kids. Anyway, the teacher made a comment about me at a parent-teacher thing, and my mom shouted at her in front of everyone. 'You're an adult! She's a child! You should be educating her, not treating her like your ex-husband'!"

Chyann laughed. "She really said that?"

Linda chuckled as well. "Yeah. After that, I always looked at her differently. She really *did* love us, in her own weird way…" Linda trailed off, her smile faltering. "She never warmed up to Buddy, though. We got him as a puppy when AJ was seven or eight. They were the absolute best of friends. Wherever AJ went, Buddy went, too. He was the sweetest dog ever." She glanced up at the window. "Dad was the normal loving parent you'd expect anyone to be. It just doesn't feel right that *Buddy* is the one who killed my parents. Or that any of them are gone at all."

"AJ is still here," Chyann said, trying to be comforting. "So are you."

"Yeah. For now."

"AJ doesn't have a rash. I think that means you're the last target. We can stop the Black Dog before it hurts you."

"I hit him with my car. I don't know what you guys are planning on doing, but I don't think he's gonna forgive and forget."

Chyann narrowed her eyes at Linda. "Does AJ know about that?"

Linda readjusted her posture and gave Chyann the side-eye. "Does it matter?"

Chyann shrugged. "Maybe. I noticed you didn't give him details about *what* attacked you and your dad. That's fine, but I also noticed he doesn't seem to know you were the one who hit him and Buddy."

"He doesn't," Linda whispered, her lip quivering. "He's all I have left, and I'm all *he* has left. I–I don't want him to hate me."

"Don't you think he deserves to know the truth?"

"Someday. But I'm not going to tell him now. He's been through too much."

An uncomfortable silence settled between them.

Chyann rubbed her hands together. "Look, I won't say anything to him, but… I don't think keeping the truth from him is a good idea." Linda met Chyann's eyes with an unconvinced glare. "The longer you go without telling him, the more it's going to hurt him when he eventually finds out. After that, he might never let you in again."

Linda remained silent, a thoughtful expression coming over her face. She seemed to be considering Chyann's words.

"Just like Willy," Chyann added.

Linda looked puzzled. "Willy?"

"Yeah," Chyann replied. "He never told me or Ryan about you. I didn't know about you guys until we saw you in the alley the other day. We don't keep secrets from each other, so whatever happened between you two must have hurt him pretty deeply."

Linda's cheeks flushed an angry shade of red. "Okay, first off," she practically spat, "I didn't do anything to him, all right? *He* broke up with *me*."

Chyann's eyes widened. She wasn't sure she'd heard Linda right. "Wait, what? He dumped you?"

"Yeah. It was sudden. He just ended things and walked away and started pretending like he never knew me."

Chyann couldn't believe this. She had assumed up until now that Linda had dumped Willy and broken his heart. He still seemed to really like Linda, so why had he broken up with her in the first place? "Did he say why?" Chyann asked.

Linda huffed and scratched her arm. "No. One minute we're having fun and sneaking out, the next he's dumping me and leaving."

Chyann leaned back in her seat. *What's going on with you, Will?*

Linda continued scratching herself. Up and down, faster and faster, the spots on her arm growing more and more inflamed.

A foul odor assaulted Chyann's nostrils, and her heart skipped a beat. She looked over at Linda. Linda slowly stopped scratching and turned to the left. Chyann followed Linda's gaze to the end of the hall.

Smoke rose up from the floor, paw prints sizzling into the tiles. The prints crept toward them, the Black Dog remaining hidden until it emerged from the smog. The monster bared its fangs and let out a low growl.

Chyann leapt to her feet and yanked the cap off the salt can. She dumped some into her palm and hurled it at the beast.

The salt hit the Black Dog. However, aside from a few miniscule embers flying out from the monster's form, the salt did nothing. Linda scrambled into a standing position and walked backward. Chyann followed the other girl's lead.

As they stepped away, the beast drew closer. "What do we do?" Linda asked, her voice barely more than a squeak.

Chyann wished she had a good answer. *Salt's no good*, she thought. *Can we outrun it? Where are the boys when I need them?*

Chyann pitched the can of salt at the dog and snatched Linda's hand. "We run!" she cried, dragging Linda down the hall as she dashed for the nearest exit.

A deafening bark echoed across the walls. Chyann glanced back and saw the Black Dog giving chase– a shadow with two glowing red eyes hurtling after them.

Chyann tugged Linda down a hall to the left. She spied a door ahead that read *Stair Access*. "This way!"

She slammed into the door and twisted the handle. Linda squeezed past Chyann into the stairwell. Chyann chanced another glance over her shoulder. The Black Dog was less than twenty feet away.

Just moments before it reached her, the door to a patient's room opened. A nurse stepped out into the hall.

The nurse didn't have a chance to react before the beast rammed into her. They tumbled to the floor. Within moments the Black Dog climbed back to its feet and turned on the woman with a vicious growl.

Chyann hurried to help, but before she could reach the nurse, a pair of hands seized her wrist and yanked her into the stairwell. The door shut behind her. A woman's scream and a wet ripping noise sounded from the other side of the door.

"What'd you do that for?" Chyann shouted as Linda pulled her down the stairwell. "That woman needed help!"

"Sorry I don't wanna see you turned into kibble next!" Linda snapped in reply.

The lights in here were dim, but Chyann could still make out the steps as they darted down them. Linda eventually released her hold on Chyann, and they continued hurrying down flight after flight.

The moment they reached the bottom of their fourth staircase, something hard collided with Chyann. The impact knocked her into a wall. She fell to the floor, and Linda screamed.

Chyann looked up. Saw the Black Dog blocking their path. Linda backed into a corner and shrieked again.

Before the Black Dog could strike, something small and dark sprinted up the stairs ahead of Chyann. It jumped toward the beast from behind.

The monster yiped and turned around. Swinging from its shadowy tail was the puppy Willy had been carting around. The puppy growled, tugging at the Black Dog with his tiny jaws.

Willy and Ryan appeared next. Willy brandished a baseball bat with thick nails driven into the top. "Yo, Fido," Willy called. He swung the bat sideways. It connected with the Black Dog's cheek.

The creature yowled, holes burning through its form. The moment reminded Chyann of Adella when Willy had struck her down with a fire poker.

Spinning around, the Black Dog flung the puppy from its tail. Willy smacked the beast's head with the bat. With another loud cry, its form burned away completely, fading from sight.

Ryan hurried to Chyann and helped her up, and Willy rested the bat on his shoulder, smirking. "You two are *so* lucky the elevator is out of order."

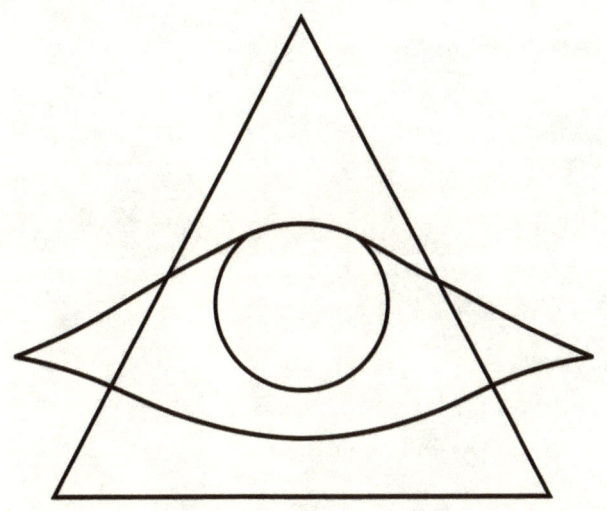

CHAPTER 6

"So here's the plan," Willy said as he helped Ryan pour rock salt in a circle around AJ's bed. "The salt should keep the big bad Black Dog away long enough for us to pass him on. Chy's gonna stay here to keep you guys safe." He finished pouring what was in his can and looked over at Linda, who sat on a chair next to AJ inside the circle.

"Will *this* stuff actually work?" Linda asked.

Ryan finished dumping his can, closing the circle. "Rock salt is purer than table salt. It's like poison to spirits. They can't cross over it."

"Please," AJ yelled, "can somebody tell me what's going on?"

Willy opened his mouth to explain, but Linda spoke up before he could. "The thing that attacked Mom and Dad is some kind of ghost. These guys are gonna stop it before it hurts us." She gave Willy a stern look. "Right, Willy?"

Willy glanced at Chyann. The other girl stood by the door keeping watch. She shrugged. Willy turned to AJ. "Yeah, exactly. Sounds crazy, I know, but trust me."

AJ shook his head. "Ghosts? Ghost *dogs*?"

Willy sat down on the bed across from Linda. "Honest truth. That nurse it swiped earlier shook-up security in this dump. I promise ya they won't find it."

AJ paused before talking again. "And you guys know how to stop it?"

Willy pointed at Chyann and Ryan. "It's kinda our job now."

"You guys fight ghosts?" AJ asked, his eyes lighting up a bit.

"And monsters, and psycho jerks in trench coats."

AJ laughed. He leaned closer to Willy and whispered, "You and Linda never should'a broke up, man."

Willy lowered his head. "Yeah, well." He met Linda's eyes for a moment. "Sometimes things just don't work out."

AJ's shoulders drooped. "Yeah…"

"But listen," Willy went on, "I know things have been hard for you and your sister. Between this"–he gestured to the room–"and your folks, and Buddy…

I'm sure it hasn't been easy. Probably the hardest thing you're ever gonna deal with." His gaze darted between AJ and Linda. "I'll get you guys through this. I promise."

"I…" AJ started. "I didn't even think about what we're gonna do next."

"You'll be fine," Willy said, standing up. "You got your big sister lookin' out for ya." He gave Linda a serious look as he uttered the last few words, but she avoided his eyes.

Without another word, Willy turned and grabbed his nail bat before heading over to Ryan and Chyann, who were near the door. Ryan had the duffel bag slung over his shoulder, which contained their short shovels and the remainder of their salt and lighter fluid. *We'll definitely need those*, Willy thought, resting the bat on his shoulder. "Are we ready to put Fido down for the second time?"

Ryan shook the bag strap. "Just waiting for you, Romeo."

"Bite me."

Chyann waggled her car keys in Willy's face. He reached for them, but she pulled them back at the last second. "Not a scratch, understand?"

He nodded. "Yeah, of course."

"Good," she said sweetly, then handed the keys to Ryan.

Willy dropped his outstretched arm. "C'mon."

"I'm *not* letting you drive until you get more practice in."

"Pfft," Willy replied, and Chyann stepped past him into AJ's room. Willy followed Ryan out into the hallway.

A soft whine sounded from behind Willy. He stopped and looked back to see the puppy watching him curiously. Willy knelt and patted the dog on the top of the head. "I'm sure you wanna tag along too, little guy, but we need you to play defense here."

The puppy whined again, then trotted over to the bed and laid down next to Chyann's foot. "Come back in one piece," Chyann said, crossing her arms.

"We will," Ryan assured her.

With that, Willy shut the door. He and Ryan glanced around the corner to make sure there were no security guards nearby, then crept toward the stairwell to leave.

It took a few minutes for the guard on the ground floor to pass, but Willy and Ryan eventually made it outside through a back exit and circled around to the parking lot.

Soon they hopped into Chyann's car. Ryan started the vehicle, then pulled out and drove off. "You ready for this?" he asked.

Willy snorted. "Dude, we've done this before."

"Yeah, with an old pile of bones. This is a dog that died a few days ago. Big difference."

Willy stared out the windshield and rested his head back against the seat. "Just step on it, will ya?"

CHYANN SAT IN A CUSHIONED CHAIR, CLOSELY watching the door to AJ's room as she grasped their last can of rock salt. Linda and AJ were quiet behind her, and the puppy lay next to her feet. Every few minutes, he let out a couple of soft whines.

Thunder *boom*ed outside. Lightning flashed in through the window, illuminating slivers of the room. *Sounds like the storm's getting worse again.*

The puppy's tail swayed side to side periodically. Finally, he released a low growl, his attention fixed solely on the door. A *bump* sounded in the hallway. Chyann picked up what could only be footsteps coming toward the room.

Linda gasped. "What–"

Chyann shushed Linda. Rising from her chair, she lifted the salt. The puppy growled again, louder this time.

Chyann tightened her grip on the can, ready to throw it at a moment's notice. She chanced a glance at the line of salt under the door. *If it can't get past that, we should be fine. Right?*

The footfalls stopped outside the door, a yellow glow peeking in through the cracks of the closed blinds. The knob turned, and the door swung open, narrowly missing the salt line on the floor.

A middle-aged man in a security uniform poked his head in, a flashlight in hand. He scanned the room, looking over everyone. "You kids okay?"

"F-fine," Chyann stammered.

The puppy barked at the guard, jumping to his paws. The guard shined his light at the dog. "Normally we don't allow pets, but I'm a bit more concerned with finding the thing that's prowling around the building than I am about him sitting in here with you." He shined the light at Chyann next. "Keep him as quiet as you can, and keep the door locked until one of us comes back to get you. Got it?"

Chyann loosened her grip on the salt can and lowered her arm. "Yeah, we got it."

"Good." The guard shuffled back into the hallway. As he closed the door, a rotten stench wafted into Chyann"s nostrils. The puppy started barking again, even louder and more frantic this time.

Chyann glanced over her shoulder to see Linda scratching her arm. Linda met Chyann's gaze with wide eyes. "It's here!"

Chyann pivoted toward the door at the sound of a man's agonized scream. *The guard*, she realized.

If the guard was in pain, it didn't last long. There was a gruesome ripping noise. Silence followed.

Chyann's pulse quickened, her mouth going dry. She raised the salt again, waiting for the beast to appear.

Seconds ticked by.

Then minutes.

No sounds found their way into the room.

No Black Dog appeared.

Chyann used her free hand to gesture at Linda and AJ. "Stay put," she said.

She crept toward the door. Behind her, the puppy growled, but he didn't follow her.

Chyann neared the door. She reached for the knob. *Maybe it doesn't know we're in here. Maybe it moved on.*

…Yeah, right.

She inched closer and closer until she could grasp the knob.

Something struck the door hard.

Shock waves arced through Chyann's hand and arm, the scent of incinerated metal permeating the air.

She stumbled back. Tripped over her foot and toppled to the floor. Looked up.

Her heart nearly stopped at what she saw.

Long black claws pierced through the metal door. The claws dragged downward, sparks fluttering around the gashes left behind.

The door *screeeeeech*ed as the claws finished shredding through the metal. Flames crackled out from the lacerations, spreading all the way to the floor. They hit the salt line and burned through it, and the claws vanished.

Chyann scrambled to her feet.

Thick smoke poured into the room through the gouges in the door, and the Black Dog strolled out of the cloud as if it were stepping through a pair of drawn curtains, its eyes glowing red. It bared its fangs, a menacing growl sounding from deep in its throat.

The puppy snarled and barked from behind Chyann. She stepped back until she stood in the salt circle around AJ's bed.

The Black Dog ambled forward and lowered its head to sniff the salt. Once it got a few good whiffs, it focused on Chyann.

"Th-th-that's the thing that k-killed Mom?" AJ stuttered.

"That's it," Linda said, her voice shaking.

The Black Dog stared hard at Chyann. No, that wasn't right. It wasn't staring *at* her. It was…

The beast released a mighty bark, thrusting everything into chaos. The sound of glass shattering erupted from behind them. Wind and rain blasted into the room with unnatural force. Chyann screamed, covering her head with her arms.

Wait, the salt! She glanced down. Sure enough, the gales were already blowing away the salt circle.

She gulped, glaring up at the Black Dog and readying the salt can. *This is bad.*

Before Ryan could even park the car, Willy jumped out and hopped the fence leading into the Blakes' backyard. *Gotta hurry*, he thought. *This thing could be attacking Chy right now.*

He slipped in the mud but found his footing, then halted beside Buddy's grave. He stabbed the blade of his shovel into the earth and dug as fast as he could. Ryan appeared next to him and started working as well.

Under rain and wind, Willy and Ryan shoveled until something white came into view. "There!" Ryan shouted.

Willy pushed more dirt away and eventually uncovered a dog-shaped sheet in the muck. The smell was strong, ten times worse than Adella.

Gagging, Willy turned around and tried to get a breath of fresh air. "Man, that's nasty." He unzipped the duffel bag to pull out the lighter fluid. "Think this stuff'll still light 'im up in the rain?"

"Not sure." Ryan set the shovel aside and traded it for a can of salt. "Only one way to find out."

The Black Dog huffed as it waited for the salt circle to blow away entirely. Chyann watched the circle grow more and more thin. Soon mere grains connected it.

The beast stomped forward, its claws burning into the floor before the salt.

Stay calm, Chyann thought. *Stand your ground. You aren't defenseless yet.*

Beside her, the puppy barked madly, as if challenging the hulking creature himself.

The Black Dog rose its haunches, preparing to leap toward Chyann.

A gust blew what remained of the salt circle astray.

The monster snarled again…

…then jerked its head to the side, its ears perking up.

Chyann's breath caught in her throat. *Did something else catch its attention?*

The beast growled and stepped away, vanishing in a cloud of smoke.

Chyann scanned the room for any signs of the Black Dog, but all that remained of its visit were the still-smoldering paw prints on the tiled floor.

"W-where did it go?" AJ asked.

Chyann allowed her shoulders to relax. "I'm not sure." And she wasn't. It had been so close to attacking her, and then it had just… left? What could have possessed it to…

Wait a second.

Suddenly it all made sense.

The boys. It's going to defend its body.

WILLY DUMPED THE LIGHTER FLUID ONTO Buddy's body while Ryan poured salt over it. Once Willy emptied the container, he set it aside and reached into the duffel bag for the matches. He located a few books of them and pulled them out.

Turning back to the pit, he spotted inky black smoke rising from the ground behind Ryan. He pointed at the smoke. "Ry!"

Ryan swung around. The Black Dog leapt out of the cloud and shoved him aside. He slammed into a tree and crashed to the ground.

Willy seized his shovel and swung. The blade *clang*ed against the beast's head. Chunks of dark sludge splattered out from it. The creature stumbled back a bit, but overall it seemed unfazed.

Snarling, it charged toward Willy. He dove to the side and splashed into the mud. His bat was just a few feet away. He crawled toward it.

A massive black paw rammed into the ground in front of him. The Black Dog swiped its claws in his direction. He rolled out of the way just in time.

As the monster raised a paw to lash out once more, Ryan appeared behind it. He pierced it through the back with his shovel blade.

The Black Dog flinched, turned its head, and released a deafening bark. As the sound reverberated through the air, Ryan's shovel snapped where the blade met the handle. The blade fell to the ground. The beast slammed into Ryan again.

Ryan flew backward. He smashed through the fence and landed in the neighbor's yard.

Willy scrambled to his bat and snatched it up. He jumped to his feet and swung. The bat bashed into the Black Dog's head.

The beast yiped and staggered over, sparks flashing where the nails had struck it. Willy reared back to swing again, but the monster ducked beneath the attack.

The Black Dog advanced and knocked Willy down. He landed hard on his spine.

He tried to stand, but the creature stepped on top of him. The whole of its weight crushed down on him.

Using both hands, Willy shoved the bat at the dog, trying to shield himself. Powerful jaws clamped down on the wood. Though his arms burned at the effort, he held the bat firm. The monster barked and thrashed with the bat in its mouth.

One of its paws connected with Willy's chest. Pain seared across his skin, the scent of burning flesh assaulting his nostrils.

The beast's claws dug in. It pierced Willy's skin.

Willy screamed, but he didn't back down, even though the monster's claws raking across his flesh hurt more than anything he'd experienced before. It felt as if all the fires of Hell were being concentrated into four points on his chest.

The Black Dog pressed down, and Willy's arms grew tired. *This is it*, he thought. *I'm a goner.*

Out of nowhere, the creature yelped. It ripped its jaws from the bat and lifted its head to the sky.

Thunder roared overhead, and the beast howled–a sorrowful sound. In moments its form burned until there was nothing left but ashes.

Though the claws disappeared from Willy's chest, the pain remained. He glanced over at Buddy's grave, saw Ryan standing over it. Flames flickered from within the pit. Ryan cradled his left arm, a distressed expression on his face as he made his way over to Willy.

Ryan offered Willy a hand. Willy accepted, and the other boy hauled him to his feet.

Willy looked down at his chest. Tiny tendrils of smoke rose from four holes in his sweatshirt. "Man, this is my favorite hoodie." He gingerly rested a hand over the wound. It was sensitive to the touch, stinging as the rain hit it.

Willy and Ryan trudged over to the grave and stared down into it. Despite the weather, the fire blazed on. *Sorry Buddy.*

Ryan motioned to Willy's chest. "You good?"

"I'm peachy."

"You're smoking, dude."

Willy patted the area, putting out a few remaining embers. "Yeah, smokin' hot."

Ryan paused, then rested an open palm over Willy's hand, the one he was patting his chest with. "Sure, Will."

Willy let out a cry of pain, but it quickly morphed into laughter. He punched Ryan's arm. "Prick."

His attention wandered back to Buddy's final resting spot. He couldn't help but feel... bad. Adella had been one thing. But Willy *knew* Buddy.

He bit his lip. "You, uhh–you think these guys go somewhere nice when we toast 'em?"

"I hope so," Ryan said.

"He wasn't a bad dog, y'know?"

"Yeah?"

"Yeah. He was super nice and friendly. Loyal as hell." Willy sighed. "Sucks it came to this."

Ryan tilted his head "Do you wanna say a few words for him?"

Willy thought it over, then bent down and picked up his shovel from the mud. "Rest easy, boy."

He dug up chunks of dirt and dropped them into the grave, snuffing out the flames.

CHAPTER 7

THE HOSPITAL WAS EVEN MORE CHAOTIC than it had been when Willy and Ryan left earlier. Animal control and patrol cars swarmed the place, making it much harder to sneak back in. The boys left their gear in Chyann's car since there wasn't much need for it now.

It took a while to reach the fifth floor because of the guards and authorities, but eventually they made it. Blood stained the tiled hallway, but the body of the person it had come from had been moved. What concerned Willy even more than the blood, however, was the door to AJ's room. *Are those claw marks?*

Willy sprinted toward the door, Ryan close behind. "Chy?" They barreled into the room. The window was shattered, broken glass littering the floor. The salt circle had been broken, thousands of little grains scattered about.

Relief flooded Willy when he saw Chyann rise from a chair next to the bed, Linda and AJ sitting behind her. Beside them, the puppy leapt to his paws with excitement.

Chyann hurried over to Willy and Ryan, the puppy on her heels. "You guys are okay!" She hugged them tightly.

Willy's chest flared with pain. He pushed her back a bit. "Easy, easy! I'm wounded."

Chyann released him and looked at his chest. "Oh my God. Does it hurt?"

"No, it feels great," he replied sarcastically.

She huffed. "Well, *excuse me* for being worried." She moved over to the cabinets and started going through them. "There's probably something in here we can use to clean it before it gets infected." Ryan winced, pressing a hand to his head.

The puppy barked at Willy. He offered the dog a smile. "Hey, boy." He knelt down, and the puppy jumped into his lap and licked his face. Despite his burning injuries, Willy laughed, patting the dog on the head. "Somebody sure missed us, huh?"

Linda walked toward Willy. "So it's over?"

"Dog's been kenneled," he said. "Permanently." She sighed in relief.

When Willy climbed to his feet again, Linda embraced him. His wounds stung as she pressed her body against his, but he couldn't help hugging her back. "Thank you," she whispered in his ear.

"Don't mention it." He stood there, holding Linda for what felt like forever, before she finally released him.

"It's all done?" AJ asked from his bed. "Just like that?"

Willy nodded. "Just like that."

"What happened to it? Why was it after us?"

Willy opened his mouth to answer, but Linda beat him to it. "We don't know. Right, Willy?"

Willy paused, glancing at AJ.

"It was just some ghost-dog thing and it wanted to hurt us for who-knows-what reason," Linda continued, scratching her arm.

Willy seized her free hand and pulled up her sleeve. The rash hadn't faded yet. "Hey guys," he called over his shoulder. "If we wasted Fido, then why's this still here?" He looked back at them. They studied Linda's rash with concern.

Before they could say a word, a horrid stench filled the room. The puppy began to bark, again and again.

A thick cloud of smoke materialized from nothing, and a dark, canine-like shape emerged from it.

The shadow headbutted Chyann. She slammed into Ryan. They tumbled to the floor in a heap.

Willy lunged toward his friends, but the shadow leapt into his path, a vicious growl sounding from its throat. Glowing red eyes bored into Willy, the monster's fangs exposed.

The Black Dog paced closer. Heart pounding, Willy put himself between the beast and Linda. The puppy stood next to Willy, growling at the creature despite their drastic height difference.

Chyann and Ryan scrambled to their feet from behind the Black Dog, watching in horror as it closed in on Willy and Linda.

"Why's it still here?" Willy shouted.

Ryan threw his hands in the air. "Maybe we missed something!"

Chyann's gaze darted between the Black Dog and AJ, who was still in bed. "Not some*thing*, but some-*one*."

Willy pushed Linda backward, shielding her with his arms. "You wanna share with the class?"

"The Black Dog isn't tied to its body," Chyann explained. "It's tied to *AJ*. That's why he never got a rash! The Black Dog didn't come back for revenge for its own death. It came back to get justice for AJ!"

"What? Me?" AJ cried, his voice laced with panic.

"Linda," Chyann continued, "you have to tell AJ the truth!"

Linda clutched Willy by the shoulder. "W-what? No!"

Chyann set her jaw. "You have to. Buddy can't rest until AJ can."

"Buddy?" AJ whispered. "What about Buddy?"

"AJ…" Linda started.

"What about Buddy, Linda?"

Linda gulped. "When you and Buddy got hit by that car, it wasn't some hit-and-run like Dad and I told you. It was… it was *me*. I wasn't paying attention to the road, and I hit you both. Now Buddy's back because he's angry!"

Willy scanned his surroundings for a weapon. The closer the Black Dog got, the more he could feel its hot breath on his face. As it walked, its feet sizzled against the floor.

Why'd I have to leave my bat in the car? What's in here that I can use for defense?

"T-that's Buddy?" AJ asked, his voice cracking.

Willy bumped into Linda. She had nowhere left to go; they were backed against a wall. "That's Buddy," Linda confirmed.

AJ swung his legs out of bed and slid himself to the floor. His balance was shaky at best, but he pressed his arm against the bed and hauled himself to his feet, then dragged himself toward the Black Dog, a familiar collar in hand.

"AJ, stay back!" Linda screamed.

"If it's Buddy, then he'll listen to me." AJ stumbled between the hulking beast and Willy and Linda. The

Black Dog halted, though it didn't stop growling. AJ's whole body trembled, though whether it was from fear or the fact that he wasn't ready to be up and around, Willy couldn't be sure.

AJ dangled the collar in front of the Black Dog. "Buddy, you have to stop." The monster barked once in reply, as if in indignation. AJ tightened his grip on the collar. "You have to stop hurting people."

The creature ceased its snarling, but its fangs remained visible. AJ inched forward. "You're scared and angry because of what happened to us. That's okay. I am too. But attacking others isn't right."

The sounds Willy heard next caught him off guard. The Black Dog began to whine, and it sounded almost... mournful.

AJ limped closer to the monster. "I know it sucks. It's not fair. But that's just how life is." The creature whined again, dropping its head as if in shame. Even from behind, Willy could see tears streaming down AJ's cheeks. *Chy was right. AJ's the only one who can finish this.*

AJ knelt before the massive black form as best he could. "You really came back for me?" The creature lowered its ears. AJ reached out with his free hand and pet its head. The boy's touch seemed to have an effect on it, but Willy couldn't quite pinpoint what that effect was just yet.

"It's okay," AJ said. "*I'm* okay." He closed the last bit of space between them and wrapped his arms around its neck. "You can rest now, Buddy."

A soft orange glow emanated from the Black Dog as AJ hugged it. Flames burned through the ectoplasm making up its form.

The fire grew brighter and brighter until it practically blinded Willy. He covered his eyes. When he lowered his arm, the beast was gone.

In its place stood Buddy. The golden retriever rested his head on AJ's shoulder. He licked AJ's cheek, his shaggy blond curls shining with supernatural light. "Thanks for always watching out for me," AJ said in a quiet voice.

Buddy barked happily. His form flickered a few times, then faded from sight, his spirit finally at rest.

AJ held his arms out in the now-empty space. The room fell silent.

Willy glanced back at Linda, and they locked eyes. She looked real mixed-up, but mostly she seemed relieved. She checked her arm. The rash was already clearing.

Willy faced his friends. They offered him sad smiles, and he let out a long breath. *It's finally over.*

EPILOGUE

WILLY SAT ON THE HOOD OF CHYANN'S CAR next to his friends. The puppy scampered across the pavement by their feet, but he never strayed too far.

The rain had finally stopped, and now the early morning sun shone down on the hospital parking lot, which was riddled with puddles.

Willy listened in on Linda and Sheriff Greyson's conversation. He asked her questions about what she knew about the attacks that had occurred over the past few days.

"You're sure?" Greyson asked, scribbling in his notebook.

"It was some kind of wolf or big dog," she answered.

"And you have no idea why it would be following you and your brother from your house to the hospital?"

"No clue."

Greyson nodded and took a few more notes before jutting his thumb at Willy, Ryan, and Chyann. "What about them?"

Linda met Willy's eyes for a moment, then focused on the sheriff once more. "They're friends from school. They came to visit me and my brother."

"And that's it?"

"That's it."

Greyson glanced over his shoulder at Willy and jotted down more information before flipping his notebook shut and putting it in his pocket. "All right," he said, facing Linda again. "We're about done here. Do you have somewhere you and your brother can stay for now?"

"We have an aunt in Cody who can take us in."

"Good. I'll give her a call and get you guys a ride figured out."

"Thank you, sir."

He tipped his hat. "Anytime, kid." He ushered her off. "You're free to go."

Linda hurried over to the trio. As she did, Willy and Greyson stared at one another. Finally, Greyson pulled out his cell phone and headed toward his truck.

Willy slid off the hood of the car when Linda reached all of them. "Thanks for not rattin' us out back there," he said.

Linda crossed her arms. "Only seems fair, after everything."

Willy scratched the side of his head. "Yeah… Uh, how's AJ?"

She shifted her feet. "He's angry. He refuses to talk to me right now, but…" She looked away and nodded. "I think he's gonna be okay. *We're* gonna be okay."

"Good. Glad to hear it."

They stood there for a bit before Linda leaned over and kissed him on the cheek. She stepped back. "Maybe we can start over again someday."

Willy grinned. "Maybe."

"Take care of yourself."

"You, too."

Linda smiled and waved at Chyann and Ryan, then turned around and started off toward the ambulance AJ sat in the back of. AJ also smiled and waved at them, but as Linda approached, he frowned and turned away.

Willy waved back but didn't move from where he stood. Something about this still bothered him.

"You think they're gonna be okay?" Chyann asked from behind him.

Willy stuffed his hands in his sweater pocket and swung around. "Those two? Definitely." He walked over to the car and leaned against it. Ryan and Chyann hopped off the hood and did the same. "They're tough as hell. They'll figure it out."

"What's wrong, then?" Chyann asked. "Why do you look so sad?"

Willy shrugged. "Just thinkin' about Buddy. He wasn't a bad dog. I mean, he came back *for* AJ."

"Not all spirits are inherently bad," Ryan said. "Some are good and just had something bad happen to them."

Willy looked back at the hospital. "You guys still wanna know?" He turned to Chyann.

She shook her head. "If you don't wanna tell us, we'll stop asking."

Ryan pressed a palm against his forehead. "Yeah, it's no big deal."

Willy grinned. "Good. That's what I've been sayin'." He took a breath. He *had* been ready to tell them. But now that they said it was "no big deal," did he need to?

For some reason, his eyes were drawn to Linda and AJ talking behind the ambulance. AJ still seemed angry, but at least he was *speaking* to his sister. That was something, right?

"We were sneakin' out together," Willy started. "We did that a few times, just to get her outta the house. This one night she was excited, feelin' real stir-crazy. Desperate to get out. She made some passing comment about how stuck-up Chy was. Not even an insult, just…" He laughed once. "Just talkin'. When I suggested she come hang with all of us at Larry's or somethin', she said she didn't wanna hang out with you guys." He shrugged. "That was that."

There was a long stretch of silence before anyone spoke again.

Chyann brushed some hair behind her ear. "So, you broke up with her because she didn't like us?"

Willy scratched his cheek. "Yup. If she can't like my friends, I can't like her. It's that simple."

Chyann and Ryan shared knowing looks. "Will," Ryan began, "you didn't have to do that. If she made you happy–"

"Who's hungry?" Willy interrupted. He motioned at his burned chest. "I dunno about you guys, but I'm tired, cold, sore, and after the night I've had, I'd say I've earned a burger." He opened the door and climbed into the back seat.

Chyann and Ryan got in as well. "Breakfast sounds good," Chyann said quietly, starting the car.

Before closing his own door, Willy leaned out and whistled. The puppy ran over and leapt into the vehicle. "Chop-chop, Doofus," Willy said.

Chyann raised her eyebrows at him in the rearview mirror. "You named him?"

"I'm *keepin'* him," Willy replied as the puppy rolled around in his lap.

Chyann drove the car out of the lot and started toward Larry's. "*You're* gonna take care of a dog?"

"Aw, come on." Willy picked up Doofus and turned him toward Chyann. "Look at those sad little eyes. How could you say no?"

Chyann huffed, but Willy could see she was smiling. He set the dog back in his lap and patted the little guy's head. After the way he'd stood up to the Black Dog, Willy figured he'd earned a spot on the team.

Ryan looked back at them. "Where are we even gonna keep him?"

Willy laughed. "At Chy's house. Duh."

BLACK

Written by:
D.R. Mills

TO BE CONTINUED IN BOOK 6
SOUL SEARCHING

*If you would like to follow D. R. Mills's journey or the **MONSTERS** series specifically, check out the author's official Twitter and Instagram accounts:*

- Instagram: @monsters_bookseries

- X: @MonstersSeries

- Facebook: @Monsters/100067554032850

- TikTok: www.tiktok.com/@monstersseries

If you enjoyed the story, dont forget to leave a review on your preferred platform! Reviews help authors find more readers, and if you'd like D. R. Mills to be able to release books faster, reviews are the best way to support him.

READ THE PREQUEL

A NOTE FROM THE AUTHOR

Hey everyone! D. R. Mills here. It's been a while, huh? This book took me a while to get out. 2024 was a rough year for me. I've been sitting on this book for pretty much the entire year, maybe longer.

I'm really proud of how this one turned out, and I'm SO excited that it's finally out in the world for everybody to read! The Willy focused ones always seem to be the most fun ones to write, and I love exploring the character hiding behind all the smart remarks and one liners.

I'm hopeful that 2025 will be a stellar year for book releases to make up for how slow 2024 was for me. If you haven't seen the announcement or news anywhere yet, I'll let you know right now–I've been hard at work on a series totally unrelated to MONSTERS, and it'll likely be the very next book I release after this one!

It's titled *Riley Doesn't Want To Fight Evil*, and it's a horror comedy following the average life of Riley Thomas, a guy who wants to do anything else besides save the world.

It's the biggest book I think I've ever written, and I'm incredibly happy with how it turned out. Keep your eyes peeled for that in the very near future. You can follow the Sea of Ink Press Blog for announcements and news, and you can even sign up for my newsletter there where you'll have access to sneak peeks at future book releases and other special goodies.

Thanks for reading, and thanks for sticking around after what a slow release year it's been.

It's good to be back on track!

-DRM

D. R. MILLS

is a young-adult horror author who is currently hard at work on his debut series, *MONSTERS*. He was born and raised in Wyoming, where he's still lurking around somewhere. When he isn't writing, he's playing video games a borderline unhealthy amount or spending time with his beautiful wife.

WWW.SEAOFINKPRESS.WORDPRESS.COM